THE STATES WITNESS 3

The Final Verdict

KYIRIS ASHLEY

URBAN AINT DEAD

URBAN AINT DEAD
P.O Box 448
Maybrook, NY 12543

Cover Design: Akirecover2cover.com

Edited By: Artessa Michele-Thomas / Editing01

Contact Author on FB: Kyiris Ashley / IG: @kyirisashley

Contact Publisher at www.urbanaintdead.com

Email: urbanaintdead@gmail.com

Print ISBN: 979-8-9888415-6-2

CONTENTS

Scan the QR Code below to listen to the Soundtracks/Singles of some of your favorite U.A.D titles:

Don't have Spotify or Apple Music?

No Sweat!

Visit your choice streaming platform and search URBAN AINT DEAD.

Currently on lock serving a bid?
JPay, iHeartRadio, WHATEVER!
We got you covered.

Simply log into your facility's kiosk or tablet, go to music and
search URBAN AINT DEAD.

URBAN AINT DEAD

Like & Follow us on social media:
FB - URBAN AINT DEAD
IG: @urbanaintdead
Tik Tok - @urbanaintdead

SUBMISSIONS

Submit the first three chapters of your completed manuscript to <u>urbanaintdead@gmail.com</u>, subject line: Your book's title. The manuscript must be in a .doc file and sent as an attachment. The document should be in Times New Roman, double-spaced, and in size 12 font. Also, provide your synopsis and full contact information. If sending multiple submissions, they must each be in a separate email. Have a story but no way to submit it electronically? You can still submit to URBAN AINT DEAD. Send in the first three chapters, written or typed, of your completed manuscript to:

URBAN AINT DEAD

P.O Box 448

Maybrook, NY 12543

DO NOT send original manuscript. Must be a duplicate.
Provide your synopsis and a cover letter containing your full contact information.
Thanks for considering URBAN AINT DEAD.

CHAPTER ONE

Nikki made her way through traffic, preparing to get off on the next exit. She was now in Jackson, Mississippi and was exhausted. Her eyes burned, and she blinked several times to lubricate the dryness. She needed to get something to eat and a bed before her head became too heavy to hold up behind the wheel. It was after midnight, and Nikki had been driving for the majority of the day. Getting off the highway, she knew her first stop had to be the gas station because she wouldn't make it anywhere else. She had four miles till empty and didn't want to run out of gas in an unfamiliar area.

Nikki walked into the gas station and went to the bathroom before heading to the counter. Her bladder was so full, it hurt. The combination of being pregnant and the amount of water she had drunk on the road had Nikki's bladder in an overflow.

She ran, having to speed up thinking she wasn't going to make it to the toilet in time. Feeling better after releasing her bladder, she made her way through the store, picking up whatever looked good to her at the moment. It was late, and Nikki didn't feel like stopping anywhere for food. She wanted to go directly to a motel, shower, and go to sleep. Once she was at the counter, Nikki let the clerk know she wanted to put sixty on pump four.

"No problem. That will be eighty-seven dollars and, thirty-eight cents," the attendant stated.

Nikki smiled and reached inside her purse for her wallet. After handing the attendant a hundred-dollar bill, she retrieved her change and walked out with her bags, headed back to her car.

"Damn, I know yo fine ass ain't out in these streets this time of night all alone. You must not be from around here!" a man with a country accent called out to Nikki.

Turning around, she saw an old school purple and gold Monte Carlo sitting on twenty-six-inch rims. She smiled more so at the car than the man in the driver's seat. Nikki looked at the man with skin so smooth and rich, it resembled dark chocolate. His freshly twisted long locs that hung in his face gave him a bad boy persona that Nikki was instantly attracted to. However, when he smiled back at her, exposing his top and bottom white gold diamond studded grillz, she knew he was one of the niggas around the hood getting money.

"What's yo name lil mama?" he asked.

"Jania," she replied, giving him the fake name on the ID she'd found in the bathroom of the gas station a few states back. Since finding all of the woman's personal information, Nikki decided to completely change her identity and become Jania Savage from here on out. The life she had as Nikki was full of pain and sorrow, so she was happy to leave it behind her and start fresh with a new name and location.

"I'm Feez, and it's nice to meet you. Feez and Jania, that shit got a nice ring to it, don't you think?"

Nikki couldn't help but laugh at his remark, thinking he was extremely blunt for them to have just met. Placing her bag of snacks in her car, Nikki began to pump her gas. Looking over her shoulder, she saw that Feez was still in his car watching her.

"You just gonna sit there and watch me?" she asked.

"Yeah, I wasn't playin' when I said this part of the city ain't safe, and, I gotta make sure you good," Feez replied, genuine with his response. Feez was a thug; however, the gentleman in him wouldn't allow him to leave a woman outside to fend for herself in such an uncouth neighborhood.

"If it's so unsafe around here, then why are you out here?" Nikki asked, honestly wanting to know.

"I mean, I'm the man in these streets, so muthafuckas know not to fuck with me. You not from around here though, so you wouldn't get that same respect. Niggas ruthless out here, and I don't want nothing to happen to you. The wrong nigga will look at you and see you as an easy target. I wouldn't feel right knowing that and still leaving you out here," Feez explained.

"Well, thank you, that's sweet. Since this is such a bad area, can you tell me where I should go to get a hotel room? I've been driving for hours and Imma pass out if I don't get any sleep soon."

Feez thought for a moment, then gave Nikki a name of a hotel that was about a fifteen-minute drive from where they were. He didn't know what it was, but something had him drawn to Nikki. Feez knew he wanted to see her again so, right after she put the address into her GPS, he asked for her number. Nikki gave it to him with no hesitation and saved his number in her phone. Feez didn't pull out of the gas station until Nikki was safe on the road headed to her hotel.

The next morning, Nikki was awakened by the ringing of her phone. Rolling over and looking at the clock, she saw it was only eight-thirty in the morning and felt as though she'd just went to sleep. Grabbing her phone off the nightstand, she saw it was Feez calling.

"Hello?" Nikki answered sleepily, confused as to why he was calling her this early.

"What it do, lil mama? Did I wake you up?" Feez asked.

"Yeah, but it's cool, what up doe?" Nikki asked, sitting up in bed and wiping the sleep from her eyes.

"Shit, a nigga hungry. I just wanted to know if you wanted to go get some breakfast."

"Feez, that's sweet of you to ask, but I don't even know you," Nikki countered.

"What you wanna know? Ask me a question and I'll tell you an answer. Besides, I thought going out for breakfast would be a great way for us to get to know each other."

Nikki thought about it for a moment. Feez seemed harmless and it was only breakfast, so it would definitely be in a public place. She also thought about the Fentanyl pills she had in her possession. She'd already been driving around with them from state to state. If the police pulled her over and found them, she would be done for, placed behind the wall for at least fifteen years. Nikki was aware of the way the legal system did black people, and she couldn't be a part of that type of injustice. Maybe Feez could get them off for her or at least point her in the direction of someone who could.

"Yeah, send me the address of the location and I'll be there," Nikki replied before ending the call.

After showering, she went to get dressed, only to remember she didn't have any clothes. Everything she had was in Cole's car, which Nikki had left abandoned at a gas station. The police had the car surrounded, and she couldn't take any chances on being caught for Cole's murder. So, she left, leaving the car exactly where she'd parked it. She'd picked up a few Walmart sweats, but nothing that was appropriate to go out to eat with Feez. Picking up her phone, she googled the closest women's clothing store. Finding a boutique only five minutes away, she headed there immediately.

Nikki picked out a white bodycon dress with a pair of silver heels and accessories. After purchasing the items, she went into the bathroom to change. When Nikki finally arrived at the restaurant, Feez was already there. He was sitting at a table wearing a plaid Burberry shirt and matching black Burberry pants. His locs were pulled back into a low ponytail and his lineup was freshly done. Nikki looked down at her outfit and instantly became embarrassed. *Damn, Imma have to step my game up the next time I see this nigga. I look like nobody's child compared to him*, Nikki thought. Walking up to the table, she greeted Feez with a smile, and he stood to his feet, holding his arms out for an embrace.

"You look beautiful," he complimented.

"Thank you. You look handsome yourself," she replied.

The waitress walked over to the table and took their drink orders, informing them she would back in a moment after they had a chance to look over the menu. Nikki looked at Feez, knowing a get-money nigga when she saw one. She only hoped he had the right connections to get her pills off.

"Have you been in Mississippi all your life?" Nikki asked in an effort to make small talk.

"Yes ma'am, all twenty-three years. What about you, where is home?" Feez asked.

"Atlanta, baby, born and raised. I'm just passing through Mississippi on my way to Cali."

"Damn, I should have known you was a thick ass Georgia

peach. I bet yo ass can cook like a muthafucka too, can't you?" Feez joked.

"Yeah, I can do a lil somethin'," Nikki laughed. "I got a question, why do they call you Feez?" Nikki asked, wondering how and why this fine ass man had such a peculiar name.

Feez chuckled a little; he knew it was coming because that was the same question he got every time he told a new person his name. "Because baby, in my line of work, I'm gon' always collect my fees. So, when a nigga see me, he know I'm there to collect."

Nikki's brow rose when she heard his answer. "And what is your line of business?"

"Let's just say I'm the CEO of these here streets of Mississippi."

"CEO, huh?" Nikki asked.

"That's right. I own a lot of properties around Jackson. A few laundry mats, houses, and a couple of clubs. You know, shit like that."

"So, if I needed something from these streets of Mississippi, could I come to you?" Nikki asked, moving in closer to Feez and lowing her voice, being sure not to be heard.

"Most definitely, I got you. What you need?" Feez asked.

"I got some Fentanyl pills I'm trying to sell. I don't sell drugs, but I'm gonna need the money. Can you help me get them off? It's not that many pills, but I know they worth some money," Nikki replied.

She didn't know anything about drugs at all, so she was

putting all her trust in a man she didn't even know. Nikki could only hope he didn't play her. With the reputation she had with men and the way they played her, she was reluctant to trust Feez. However, the money she could make from the pills outweighed any doubt she had in her mind.

"Fasho Jania, I got you, baby. That ain't no thing. We can get them off after we eat if you want to."

"Really? Just like that?"

"Yeah, just like that. Long as you ain't the police, we good," Feez joked.

"Nah, I definitely ain't twelve," Nikki replied.

Once they were done eating, the two walked out the restaurant and headed to their vehicles. Feez told Nikki to follow him and led her to a spot not too far from where they were. Nikki watched Feez get out of the black Land Rover he was driving and walk over to her car.

"How many pills you got?" Feez asked, wanting to see the product before he went in for the sale.

Nikki reached into her purse, pulled out a baggie filled with Fentanyl tablets and handed them to Feez. Looking down at the bag and smiling, he told Nikki to stay in the car and wait for him to return. She agreed as she turned on her radio and listened to music as she awaited his return. *I knew my luck was about to change,* Nikki thought.

"See, baby, mommy told you I was gonna make it work. We bout to be living good," she said as she rubbed her stomach.

About fifteen minutes later, Feez returned back to Nikki's car and got into the passenger seat. Reaching into his pocket, Feez pulled out a wad of money and handed it to her. Nikki's eyes widened when she wrapped her hand around the large stack of bills.

"That's seven racks. You had five grams of Fentanyl, and he pays fourteen hundred a gram," Feez stated.

Nikki quickly counted off a thousand from her stack and handed it to Feez. She was grateful to him for helping her and, although it wasn't much, Nikki felt obligated to give him something.

"Nah, lil mama, you ain't gotta do that; it ain't no thing," Feez replied, declining Nikki's money. It wasn't a big deal for him to get off a few pills for her. That was light work compared to the business he dealt with on a daily basis, and he didn't want her to feel like she owed him anything.

"Well, it's a big thing to me. Without you, I would have never gotten them pills off. I owe you at least this," Nikki replied.

"I'll tell you what, lil mama, keep yo money. I got something way better. It's a way we can both get to some real money. You said you really needed them seven racks and that's cool but, if you fuck with me, them same seven racks will be lunch money in just a few weeks."

Nikki shook her head quickly. This conversation sounded all too familiar to her, and she wouldn't fall victim to the same thing twice. Russell had promised her tons of money and a lavish lifestyle, only to have her living in hotels fucking ten plus men a day. There was no way she was going to have a round two of that. She'd overcome too much and was never going down that same road again.

"Nah, I'm good. You ain't bout to be pimping me out. I know how the game go, and I ain't selling no pussy for no nigga," Nikki shot back.

"Well, that's good because I ain't sellin' no pussy, either. Pimpin' ain't my get down. I don't knock nobody hustle, but that just ain't how I make my money," Feez replied, looking Nikki directly in the eyes so that she would know he was telling the truth.

Nikki turned beet red in embarrassment as she used her hand to cover her mouth. She hoped she'd not offended him.

"I'm so sorry Feez, I didn't… well, I only… I mean you said…" Nikki didn't know what to say as she stumbled over her words. Here this man was, didn't know her from Adam and had already helped her acquire seven thousand dollars. Now, Nikki had opened her mouth and insulted the only person who had ever really helped her.

"I hope I haven't offended you in any way?" Nikki asked.

"You good, lil mama. I tell you what, why don't you meet me later on tonight? You can meet the rest of my crew and we can explain to you what we do. Does that sound like a plan?" Feez asked.

"Sure, just text me the location."

Feez nodded and exited Nikki's car. He didn't know why

but he trusted her already. The vibe she gave off let him know she was a down ass bitch. Although he didn't know what it was, he knew she was going through some rough times and wanted to help with whatever it was. He met her at the right time because he was looking for a female to join his team. He just hoped she was down to get to the money.

Nikki made her way to the mall, knowing she needed to go shopping if she was going to see Feez again. He made her want to step her fashion game up, so there she was walking through the mall going in and out of stores. She didn't know where they would be going, so she decided she would purchase two outfits. Something casual and something more upscale, so she would be ready for anything he laid out to her. Nikki also stopped at Mac, so she could grab a few products. She was going all out just to see Feez one more time.

Girl, what the fuck are you doing? You don't even know this nigga, you better slow yo ass down, Nikki thought, feeling a bit silly. She had never felt butterflies for any man, and the fact she was feeling them for a man she'd just met had her shaking her head. Yet and still, Nikki made her way into the beauty supply store. One thing about growing up with a crackhead for a mother meant Nikki had to learn to make herself look good. There were no Saturday morning salon appointments growing up in Nikki's household. When she wanted her hair done, the most her mother would do was steal what she needed. The styling part was completely up to Nikki. After years of doing her own hair, she could do just about any style.

Getting everything she needed, Nikki headed back to her hotel, trying to catch a nap before it was time for her to get dressed.

NIKKI AWOKE from her nap around six that evening and started her hair. Feez had not texted her yet, so she figured she was making good timing. After gluing in her tracks, Nikki cut and curled her hair, styling it to perfection. Placing a shower cap over her freshly done hair, she showered and placed Nair over the areas that grew unwanted hair. Feeling smooth as a baby's bottom, Nikki got out the shower, dried off before applying her Shea Butter, and beat her face to the Gods. She had just finished applying her false lashes when she received a text. Already knowing who it was from, she opened it and got the address to the location where she would be meeting Feez. Googling the address and seeing it was a night club, she went with the blue and white Marine Serre minidress she'd purchased a few hours prior.

Once she was dressed, Nikki looked at herself once more in the mirror, amazed at the way she'd put herself together. She'd never looked this good before, and she didn't know if it was the pregnant glow or the glow of freedom. Whatever it was had Nikki feeling herself. Grabbing her keys and her purse, she left the hotel room eager to see Feez.

The line at the club was extremely long, running halfway

down the block. Feez had texted Nikki, informing her to call him once she was outside and she did so, thinking he'd held her a place in line. To her surprise, Feez sent one of the bouncers of the club out to come get her. The many dirty looks and shouts she got for being able to bypass the line had Nikki smirking the entire walk to the door. *Damn, Feez must really be that nigga,* Nikki thought.

"Who the fuck that bitch think she is? That hoe just got here and needs to wait in line just like the rest of us. I been standin' out here for forty-five fuckin' minutes," Nikki heard one woman say as she walked pass.

Normally, Nikki wouldn't have said a thing, just walk right pass her, but tonight was different. Nikki was feeling herself, so she wasn't letting shit slide. In true diva fashion, she stopped, turning around with her hand on her hip before responding, "I'm going inside, only mediocre bitches such as yourself wait in lines."

All the men around in ear shot laughed because they knew Nikki was telling the truth, while all the women in ear shot scoffed and rolled their eyes for the same reason. Nikki knew it was a cheap shot, but she didn't care; the woman should have kept her mouth closed. Nikki looked at the woman that stood there in a pair of black leggings and red bustier that she clearly picked off the twelve-dollar rack at Rainbow and dared her to say something else. When no words came from her lips, Nikki chuckled and continued to follow the bouncer to the door.

Nikki was surprised to see the club only had a handful of people inside. The way the line was damn near wrapped around the building, she thought it would be packed from wall to wall. As she looked around the beautifully decorated club, she spotted Feez and his crew sitting in the VIP area. The blue and purple strobe lights danced off his deep chocolate skin, making him look as though he could glow in the dark. The bouncer led her over to Feez, and he stood to greet her.

"Damn, lil mama, you look good as hell," Feez complimented, moving closer to Nikki and bringing her in for an embrace. The scent of her Mark Jacobs perfume invaded his nostrils.

"Thank you, you look very handsome yourself," Nikki replied.

Taking her hand, Feez walked her over to the couch where she sat next to him. The table in front of them was filled with chicken wings, lamb chops, and an assortment of brown liquor and champagne. The vibe was nice, and it was a good change of scenery for Nikki.

"Jania, let me introduce you to everybody; this is Poncho, Regal and Demo," Feez introduced, pointing to each one as he named them. Poncho was a short, brown-skinned man with hair down his back that he kept braided into ponytails. Regal was a tall, light-skinned man with a low creaser and a mouth full of gold teeth, while Demo was a dark-skinned man with cornrows. Nikki smiled and greeted the three men.

"And this thick ass fine lil thang is my girl, Shayla," Demo introduced.

"Hey girl," Shayla greeted, extending her hand for Nikki to shake. Shayla was a beautiful woman with skin that resembled butter pecan ice cream. The black Mugler pantsuit she wore looked as though it was painted on, and the white bralette she sported underneath was a nice added touch. The group chatted over appetizers as they got to know one another.

"Can someone point me in the direction of the ladies' room?" Nikki asked, speaking loudly over the music.

"It's right down that hall." Feez pointed.

Nikki nodded before standing and walking off.

CHAPTER TWO

Nakia sat in the waiting room of the same hospital where she was a patient just a few months prior. Jalyn's blood stained her shirt and hands as tears stained her cheeks. She'd refused to even wash her hands because she felt that his blood was the only thing she had left of him. She was completely broken and felt like she would never be whole again. Nakia had never known pain like this before and felt as though she would be crushed under the weight of it. She had lost her parents and the father of her two oldest children, who she thought was the love of her life, but to lose her brother, her only brother, which was a pain that Nakia didn't know how to deal with.

From the time he was born, it had just been him and her. She had raised him as her own son and gave him whatever he needed and, now, she couldn't. Nakia knew it should have been her that had been shot. Hell, the bullet was meant for her anyway, but it was Jalyn that took it. He didn't even have anything to do with the situation. Yet, somehow, he'd been the one to lose his life.

She had never imagined a life without Jalyn and had no idea how she would go on without him. How would she tell her children? Jalyn had been more than just an uncle to them; he'd been like a father. The bond Jalyn and Rashaud shared was one Nakia wished she had with someone when she was his age and, now, it had been ripped away. She was happy that Simone had come to pick the kids up while she went to the hospital. However, she was sad she was there alone without any family support. She'd tried calling Raphael a few times and all calls were left unanswered. She knew he was still upset with her for everything that happened, but she needed him now more than ever and wished he would answer her calls.

Special Agent Scott stayed at the hospital with Nakia and helped her answer the questions the local police had for her. He knew she was hurting, and he sympathized, but that didn't take from the fact he had a job to do. The reason he'd come to Nakia's house in the first place was to let her know that Russell was in jail and his trial date was moved up. She had been dodging his calls for weeks, so he decided to make a home visit. Luckily, for Nakia, he did because she might have been shot right along with her brother.

"Do you want me to give you a ride home or to a friend's house?" Agent Scott asked.

Nakia didn't say a word, just nodded with tears still streaming down her face. She felt like a failure; she'd failed her children, she failed Raphael and, most of all, she'd failed Jalyn. He was the one who told her to stay out of it, told her to mind her own business and not involve herself by calling the police. However, she didn't listen. She'd went against everything he'd told her and, now, Jalyn was the one who paid the ultimate price by losing his life.

Agent Scott walked alongside Nakia as they made their way to his car. He felt bad for her, but he had to let her know she must be in court for the trial. This was the part of the job he hated; it was clear this woman was in no position to testify; however, she had no choice. If they wanted to lock Russell up and give him the time he deserved, then she would have to do her part and testify.

"Nakia, I'm sorry for your loss, I really am; however, I have to tell you that the trial date has been pushed up. Russell was arrested and is back in custody on similar charges, so the trial will be starting Monday. We're going to need both you and Bailey to be at the 36th District court at eight in the morning," he stated.

Nakia didn't have the energy to do or say anything. The fact he was even bringing this up after she'd just lost her brother let her know that he only gave a damn about one thing. It was because of this very trial that her brother was dead, and here was the police not giving a fuck about the murder of yet another black man. Nakia's blood boiled as anger shot throughout her body.

"Pull over," she whispered.

"What?" Agent Scott asked.

"Pull the fucking car over! I just lost my fuckin' brother, and all you over here thinkin' about is a fuckin' trial? Fuck that trial and fuck you! I'd rather walk home than to be in this car with you for another second!" Nakia yelled. "Where the fuck were you and the police when he had someone break into my house and damn near kill me and baby? Y'all want me to testify in the trial of a man that has taken my entire life away from me. Y'all don't give a shit about fuckin' up anybody's lives, as long as y'all get what y'all want. You don't give a fuck who dies in the process. So, like I said, fuck that trial and fuck you!" Nakia continued.

Agent Scott looked over at Nakia in utter shock, clearly unaware of the dangers Nakia had faced. He saw the tears falling from her eyes, and his heart softened. "What do you mean he had someone break into your house? I wasn't notified about any of this," Agent Scott stated truthfully. "And what do you mean almost killed you and your baby? Did you call the police? Nakia, this is exactly why you need to testify. Russell is dangerous and needs to be off the streets. When did this happen?" he continued.

Nakia couldn't even look at him; everything was too much. She didn't give a fuck about that damn trial or Russell being on or off the streets. He'd sent someone for her so, prison or no prison, he could do that again. Nakia's only concern was her now deceased brother. The fact that he was still even talking to her about the trial was making her want to do things to Agent Scott that would land her in prison too.

"Now, I know about an incident with Bailey but not one with you. So, if something has happened, you need to tell me exactly what it was. That's the only way I'll be able to help you, Nakia," Agent Scott further went on.

"Nothing, damn! Can you just take me home or pull over? My fuckin' brother is never coming back! I still have his blood on me, and all you can talk about is Russell and this fuckin' trial? Has being a special agent made you completely heartless or were you always this way?" Nakia yelled.

Donovan Scott hated this part of the job. This woman was clearly heartbroken, and he looked like a dickhead coming to her about a trial on the same day her brother had taken his last breath. He didn't mean to be this way; he just had a job to do, so that was what he was doing.

"I'm not gonna let you walk home. It's late and I would just feel more comfortable if I saw you to your door safely. Especially with everything that transpired at your house today. We both know it's not safe for you to be alone out here. I know you're going through a lot, and I'm sorry for your loss. I'm not trying to be insensitive at all; I just need to inform you of the changes. However, my first priority now is your safety so, if something has happened Nakia, maybe we need to look into getting you into witness protection."

Ain't no way I'm going into anyone's witness protection. Agent Scott was less than a hundred feet from us when Jalyn was shot. And he still died and the shooter got away. He has already proven to me he can't protect a damn thing, Nakia thought, ready to tell Agent Scott just where he could go.

"Nothing happened," Nakia answered, keeping her eyes on the road as if she was the one driving.

"Well, okay, if you don't want to tell me, then I won't be able to do anything about it. I will say, we have a car arranged to pick of you and Bailey and bring you both to court while the trial is going on. Now that you know that information, we can continue this ride in silence," Agent Scott informed.

By the time Nakia got home, the police had finished their investigation of the crime scene and had even opened the street up to the public. Nakia's heart ached as she looked at the very spot where Jalyn had taken his last breath. She felt as though she was ready to take hers. How was this fair? All their lives they'd done everything together and, now, here she was able to breath and walk the earth, and he couldn't. She felt like she was doing something wrong. All she wanted was her brother back; however, that was the one thing that she couldn't have.

Nakia walked into her home and went up to her bathroom. Blood stained her clothes and hands, her brother's blood, and she was finally about to wash it off. Tears flowed down her face like continuous rivers, as she watched Jalyn's blood run down the drain. She felt as though she was washing his memory away and she couldn't take it, as she dropped to her knees and cried loudly. Her entire soul ached and she felt as though she couldn't breathe. *This is all my fault, this should have happened to me, not you, Jay. I should be the one dead right now*, Nakia thought as her tears mixed with the water and blood, falling down the drain as well.

Once Nakia was finally able to get herself together enough to get out the shower, she decided to pack a bag and head over to Simone's house with her children. There was no way she was gonna stay in her house alone after everything that happened, so Simone's house was the best place for her. Walking back into the bedroom area of her master suite, she placed another call to Raphael. This time, however, his phone went straight to voicemail. Hanging up and placing another call to Rosa, Nakia was happy when she heard her voice say hello.

"Rosa, where is Raphael? I need to speak with him, it's very important," Nakia cried.

"Nakia, I'm sorry, but Raphael does not want to speak with you. He already told me if you called to tell you he wasn't around. He loves you, Nakia; he just needs some time to process everything that happened. I'm sure he doesn't really blame you for our parents' murders; he's just hurt right now. I hope you understand," Rosa informed.

"Jalyn is dead," Nakia blurted out, still not believing the words as they left her lips.

"What? What the hell do you mean?" Rosa asked. The

statement caught her off guard, and she didn't understand why Nakia would say something so horrible. She'd just saw Jalyn a few hours ago, so there was no way he was dead.

"He's dead. We were outside when you and Raphael left. A car pulled up and shot at us; Jalyn took the bullets," Nakia stated.

Rosa felt like her entire world had just shifted. Here she was on a mission to find the muthafucka that killed her parents when she was just informed that her lover had been murdered as well. Rosa's head began to spin, and she sat on the couch in an effort not to pass out.

"Was it Manny?" Rosa asked, fury evident in her tone.

"I don't know what he looks like, but I'm sure it was. Ain't nobody else gonna just be shooting at me like that. Unless that nigga Russell sent somebody else after me," Nakia stated.

"Russell? What does Russell have to do with any of this?" Rosa asked, confused. "Never mind, I'm on my way to your house. I'm bringing Raphael with me," Rosa stated before ending the call.

Nakia could hear that she was crying and knew she was hurt as well. Nakia was just happy that Raphael was going to come with her. She needed him now more than ever and knew he was the only thing that could make her feel even a little bit better in that moment. She still packed a bag because no matter who was with her, there was no way she was staying in that house.

. . .

"WERE THE KIDS HURT? Where are they now? What else did she say?" Raphael asked as he weaved in and out of traffic in an effort to get to Nakia as quick as possible. He could have fucked himself up for leaving his family alone while a war was going on. Just like that, Nakia could have lost them as well.

"All she said was Jalyn was dead. A man drove up on them and shot at them. That's all the information I have," Rosa replied.

Raphael had left in such a hurry that his security wasn't even informed that he was leaving. The only one who knew was Blue, and that was only because he was with Rosa when she got the call. If it wasn't for that, he wouldn't have known either. Blue sat in the back seat ready for whatever, as Raphael allowed his speedometer to reach the triple digits.

Within ten minutes, Raphael was pulling into his driveway and running into his house, screaming out to Nakia. His heart pounded in his chest as adrenaline rushed through his body. He needed to assure his children were safe. He swore if anything was to happen to any of the kids, he would kill everything moving. There was too much murder going on around him, and Raphael knew he had to be the one to stop it. Running into their bedroom, be opened the door to their en-suite bathroom, finding Nakia sitting on the floor in a towel with her back against the wall.

"Baby, I'm so sorry," Raphael said, falling to his knees in front of her. He grabbed Nakia and pulled her into him, cradling her in his arms while rocking her back and forth like a small child.

Nakia cried loudly in his arms, and he cried too. Their emotions were through the roof and, although Raphael was still upset with Nakia, he knew they both needed each other in that moment. Leaning forward, Raphael grabbed her robe off the rack and wrapped Nakia in it, replacing the towel she was wrapped in with her plush Versace robe. Her body was freezing, and he wanted to warm her to prevent her from catching a cold.

"Nakia, where are the kids?" Raphael asked.

"They're at Simone's house," she replied weakly, her voice cracking with every word.

Nakia's entire body hurt, and she felt as though her life was coming to an end as well. She had no idea how to live without Jalyn because she'd never had to before. The pain of knowing she would never be able to call her brother or see him walk through her front door again was eating at her. She knew this was all her fault and she felt the only thing she could do was take her own life and join Jalyn in death.

"We need to get you over there too. I need to make sure y'all are safe before I can completely focus on getting at Manny. He's the one behind all this, and I swear to you I'm gonna kill him. But I can't do that if I'm walking around worried about y'all," Raphael announced.

"Okay," Nakia replied. She didn't have the energy to say anything else.

Raphael spotted the bag that Nakia had packed sitting on a chair in the corner of their room. He handed Nakia a pair of sweats to put on and some underwear from one of her drawers. She could barely stand up and Raphael saw that so, like the loving fiancé he was, Raphael helped her dress. Raphael looked at Jalyn like he was his own brother, so he was hurt by this as well; however, he was worried about Nakia. He'd never seen her like and it pained him to do so.

Taking a gun from his waist and a box of bullets from his nightstand, he placed them inside the bag he packed and made sure to tell Nakia it was in there. He wanted to make sure Nakia and their children were protected and, since he couldn't be there to do it, he wanted to assure Nakia would be able to protect them if need be.

"I'll be right back," Raphael spoke before leaving the room.

"He's really gone huh?" Rosa asked once Raphael made it back downstairs. She looked at him in anticipation, praying he would tell her it wasn't true, that this was just some type of horrible lie Nakia made up just so he would come back to her. However, when Raphael dropped his head low and shook it, she knew it was real.

"Man, sis, shits fucked up. I don't know how Nakia is gonna come back from this; Jalyn was like her first-born child.

She up there out of it, sis. I just don't know what to do," Raphael announced.

Rosa looked at Raphael confused, as if she was trying to process what he was saying to her. Before Raphael could say anything else, Rosa dropped down to her knees and cried, not being able to handle any more death. Just a few short hours ago, she was wrapped in Jalyn's strong arms, thinking about how she was falling in love with him and now, he was dead. Life had been throwing real punches at her and every one of them were landing.

"I'm gonna kill Manny, I know his ass is responsible for all this shit. He took them all from me! I promise that mutha-fucka got some shit comin' his way 'bout this. I gotta live without my mama, my daddy and my man? Oh, he got me fucked up!" Rosa cried as she pounded her fist on the hard-wood floor.

Raphael looked at Rosa confused when he heard the phrase 'my man' come from her lips. He figured she was so emotional that she didn't know what she was saying. That was, until she continued.

"I was just making that man breakfast. Looking into his eyes ready to tell him I was falling in love with him and, now, he's gone? I'm gonna fuckin kill Manny!" Rosa screamed.

"Rosa, hold up; you and Jalyn had somethin' going on?" Raphael asked.

"We had love going on, and Manny took all that away from me, right along with my fuckin' parents! I swear to you, I won't rest until that muthafucka has suffered!" Rosa screamed.

Raphael's heart broke for the fourth time that day as he watched his sister grieve the loss of her parents and her boyfriend. He wanted to kill Manny himself just off the way his sister was laid out on the floor crying. However, he knew it wasn't only Manny he had to get; his beef was with Russell as well. Raphael's trigger finger itched as he thought about the terrible things he was going to do to them both once they were found.

"I know it's hard sis, but we gonna get those muthafuckas, I promise you that shit. But, right now, we gotta get Nakia to Simone's house. She needs to be with the children because if anything happens, nobody is going to protect them like her," Raphael stated.

Seeing Raphael's point of view, Rosa nodded her head and stood to her feet. She knew she had work to do, and she couldn't do that if she was lying around crying. She wasn't gonna be one of those people who let grief consume her. Rosa was gonna take this hurt and turn it into revenge and receive her get-back. She was prepared to wreak havoc on everyone involved. Rosa didn't give a fuck if she would have to ride out alone, she would do so for her parents and Jalyn.

"I'm ready," Rosa said, standing to her feet and wiping her tears.

Rosa knew the life her family led and, although she had been kept away from it, it was still in her blood. Murder was like second nature in her family and, if she had to follow in her mother and father's footsteps, she was gonna do it with pride. Rosa watched, as Raphael ran upstairs to get Nakia. Blue was already outside waiting in the car for them, and Raphael had sent the other goons to look for Manny. They had strict orders not to kill him and to bring him to Raphael and Rosa. Once they were all inside the car, the foursome made their way to Simone's house.

CHAPTER THREE

Tianna and Tiny touched down in Detroit that afternoon and went directly to the Airbnb they'd rented. The spacious three-bedroom home was nice and also had a home office, which would definitely be utilized. After picking their rooms, they both took showers and naps, needing desperately to recharge their energy.

"Good evening, friend, nice of you to finally come out that room. We need to take us some new pictures and start up another website for Detroit. I can see if I can still log into my old one but, if not, we gotta start one," Tianna stated once Tiny walked into the kitchen.

"Girl, this baby got me tired as fuck. Plus, I didn't get no sleep on that bus ride so, once my head hit that pillow, it was over."

"Yeah, I feel you, but now it's time to get to work," Tianna replied.

Tianna had never been pregnant before; however, she'd read about the changes the female body went through during pregnancy. The way Tiny would throw up after damn near everything she ate had Tianna rethinking having children at all. At four months, Tiny still didn't have much of a stomach; however, Tianna knew it was only a matter of time before she wouldn't be able to work at all.

After setting up the website and taking various photos, the two of them relaxed in the living room, watching TV until they received their first call of the night. Tianna felt good being back in her city again, and she knew she would make ten times the money she'd made in New York. Being back on her home turf gave her a comfort that New York didn't offer, and Tianna always worked best where she felt comfortable.

When their phone vibrated alerting them of their first hit, a smile spread across Tianna's face as dollar signs flashed through her mind. She read through the email and saw the man wanted their threesome special. Tianna and Tiny had decided to take it up a notch and add a few other services such as S&M and a build your own package that included three services of the client's choice. The added features would hopefully deem to be lucrative for the two women.

After freshening up and getting dressed, they waited on the john to arrive. With this being their first client in the city, Tiny was eager to see how it would play out. Tianna had told her about the many ballers and hustlers the city had to offer, and she couldn't wait to see all the money she racked in.

Seeing how they'd gotten off to a late start, they'd only made four thousand before the sun came up. However, that was still a good payout for only having worked a few hours. Once their work day was over, the two went to their rooms. Tianna laid in bed watching TV, dozing in and out of sleep when her cell phone beeped, alerting her of a text message. Opening her messages, she read the text from the number she didn't recognize.

You still working?

Once Tianna replied back with her hours of operation, she didn't receive any more texts from the number. Not thinking anything was out of the ordinary, Tianna rolled over and went to sleep.

Tiny slept in, waking up at eleven thirty that next morning and going right into the kitchen to find something to eat. She knew there was nothing in the fridge; however, she looked anyway out of habit. Walking back into her room and taking a quick shower, she dressed in sweats, ready to head to the grocery store. Pulling up the Lyft app on her phone, she typed in the nearest Kroger and waited for the app to find her a car.

"Where you going?" Tianna asked as she walked past Tiny's open room door. She was heading to the home office to edit some of the pictures the two of them had taken for their website. She wanted to get an early start, so they would have a full day of working. Tianna had money on her mind, and nothing was going to get in the way of that. She'd come a long way, and there was nothing she wouldn't do to assure she was never in that space again.

"I'm going to the grocery store. We did a lot of eating out while we were in that motel so now that we have a kitchen, I'm gonna be cooking. It's been way too long since I've had a good ass home cooked meal. I'm talking fried chicken, mac and cheese, maybe some collard greens with a little corn bread on the side," Tiny said, rubbing her stomach and licking her lips.

"Damn bitch, that sounds good as hell. Hook that shit up," Tianna laughed before walking away.

Ten minutes later, Tiny was walking out into the black Impala that Lyft had sent her. The older white man smiled at her as she opened the door, showing all thirty-two of his coffee-stained teeth. The Cool Water cologne he wore damn near choked Tiny, as she closed the car door. *Damn, you supposed to spray that shit, not bathe in it,* Tiny thought while rolling down the window and taking in the fresh air.

"It says here that you're going to Kroger? We should be there in about ten minutes," the driver said.

This was Tiny's first time in Detroit but, as she looked out the window, it looked like every other hood. The small community where they rented the Airbnb was beautiful with huge houses and nicely cut grass. However, as soon as you turned into the main road, it was just like any other hood she'd ever seen. From the abandoned homes to the potholes, it was the same thing no matter what city you were in.

"Are you from the area?" the driver asked, making small talk.

"Nah, I'm not, just moved here," Tiny replied, still looking out the window.

"Oh really? You should take my number down just in case you need someone to show you around the city."

Tiny didn't reply, just continued to look at the many liquor stores they passed in the short distance to the grocery store. She was not in the mood to be hit on; all she wanted to do was get her shopping done and go back home. She dealt with nasty men she didn't want to talk to on a daily basis while working; she would be damned if she did so on her own time.

"There are a few concerts that's scheduled downtown in the next upcoming weeks, maybe we can go see a few. They also have festivals and a lot of good restaurants as well. Detroit is really coming up; hell, downtown feels like an entire new city. We can exchange numbers and set something up for this weekend, maybe?" the driver asked, clearly not caring that Tiny wasn't paying any attention to him whatsoever.

"That's sweet, but no thank you. I'm not looking for any new friends at the moment," Tiny declined.

Tiny could see the driver's face turn red in embarrassment as she declined his offer, staying quiet the rest of their drive. Once she got to Kroger, Tiny walked around the store filling the basket with everything that looked good to her. When they were in the brothel, they were never able to choose their food, having to eat whatever was given to them. They were only allowed one meal a day and, if they didn't like the meal, they would starve. So, with that, Tiny went overboard with the groceries, having a cart full of items for only herself and Tianna.

Eight hundred dollars later, Tiny was pushing her cart outside to wait on her Lyft. The cart was so full of grocery bags that she could barely see in front of her. She thought about the many meals she could prepare with all the food she'd bought while she waited for her Lyft to arrive. Much to her dismay, the same Lyft driver pulled up to pick her up, hopping out his car quickly to open his trunk and help Tiny with her groceries.

"Thank you," she spoke.

"We have to stop meeting like this. Me picking you up twice in one day must be some type of sign," he encouraged.

Tiny rolled her eyes, thinking the man was laying it on too thick. There was no way she was going to go out on any dates with this man. He wasn't her type at all and, on top of that, she was pregnant and not yet over the death of her child's father. However, if he wanted to pay her for her time, that could definitely be arranged. Reaching into her crossbody bag, she pulled out one of the business cards she and Tianna had made with their website information and handed it to the man.

"If you want to see me again, you can contact me here and set up an appointment," she said with a smile.

The man's eyes widened as he looked at the sexy pictures on the business card, already knowing what Tiny was selling. His dick stiffened as he looked from the card to Tiny and back to the card again. Tiny chuckled to herself, knowing she would be hearing from the man sooner rather than later.

"I'M NOT GONNA sugar coat anything. They have a lot of physical evidence against you that I thought they wouldn't have this close to trial. This isn't looking good. I've looked over your case file several times and I have yet to find any loopholes. As your attorney, it is my job to advise you on how to proceed moving forward. Now, we can take this to trial if you want, you have the right to have a fair trial; however, I suggest that you just take the deal they offer you," Kyree spoke as he thumbed through Russell's case files while shaking his head.

"Nah, I ain't takin' no plea. They tryin' to offer me sixteen years, fuck kinda deal is that?" Russell countered. He was gonna take his case to trial no matter what anyone said. He was paying his lawyer good money to get him out of this situation, so Russell was going to get his money's worth.

Kyree looked at Russell in disbelief. *This dude can't possibly be this stupid,* he thought to himself. Kyree was trying to tell Russell what was going on without actually saying it. He knew how dirty these prosecutors could get when they were trying to win a case. Although illegal, Kyree knew of cases where they had put a hidden camera in the room while lawyers spoke with their clients.

"I highly advise against that. From what the prosecution has drawn up in their file, they have several witnesses that will testify against you and an entire task force. Taking this case to trial would not be good for you. You may come out having to do more years than they offered you in the plea if we lose this," Kyree stated.

Russell didn't give a damn about any of that, and it seemed as though what Kyree said went right over his head yet again. There was no way he was just going to offer up years of his life to be in prison.

Kyree leaned closer to Russell and looked around, lowering his voice to a whisper before he continued, "I thought you said you were getting the witnesses taken care of? The names I gave you are still on the list of witnesses against you."

"What? Ain't no fucking way they got no witnesses other than that punk ass task force that tried to trap me. Any witness that can connect me to any underaged girls are dead, and I'm sure of that. We gonna take this shit to trial and fight it. And you, my friend, are going to do the job I'm paying you to do and get me out of this shit," Russell whispered.

Kyree couldn't do a thing but roll his eyes. It was mutha-fuckas like Russell that made his job hard. All Russell had to do was listen, and he was having a hard time doing that.

"Listen, as your attorney, it is my job to give you the best legal advice possible. Now, I know this is your freedom on the line, but you are not the only one that has something to lose. My reputation is also on the line with this case. I have never lost a case my entire career. I'm sure you know that, which is why you hired me. I was the one that gave you the names of those witnesses so, if anyone was to find that out, I would get disbarred. This is not only your life on the line. You want me to take on an unwinnable case when I am trying to tell you that a plea deal is the best thing for the both of us," Kyree said, clearly getting aggravated.

"Like I said, I'm not taking the plea. You can do your job or I can hire someone else to do it for you. "The choice is yours," Russell spoke before calling for the guard to take him back to his cell.

Russell knew that it was only certain charges that would stick if his case went to trial, so there was no way he was taking a plea deal. They couldn't tie him to any of the under-aged girls because every witness for that case was now six feet under, or so he thought. Now, all he would have to do was place a call to Fatbar and have him eliminate Deja and her girls. Russell had really started to like Deja and her crew, feeling like they were starting to become more of a family than business partners. Imagine his surprise when he found out that they were a taskforce built to take him down. The deception had deemed almost heartbreaking. On top of him losing Hannah, the bitch he'd put her on the backburner for was the opposition. Russell could only shake his head thinking about it as he took a seat on his cot.

That bitch gonna be the next to go! I trusted her and she played me, set me up to be put in a fuckin box. I swear Imma get that bitch touched; I don't give a fuck about her being no damn police. Russell was livid as he thought about Deja's betrayal and vowed to make a call to Fatbar as soon as he got his phone time.

Russell knew he was taking his case to trial. Both witnesses the prosecution had from the hotel were dead and, once he got a hold of Fatbar, the taskforce would be too. His lawyer was just going to have to trust the process. As soon as they opened his cell, Russell made his way over to the phones. The lines were starting to form, so Russell walked faster to assure he got a good place in line. He'd just made it to the line when a group of four men walked up to him.

"Say nigga, this my place in line, you best get behind us, fuck you thought?" one of the men said.

Russell just looked at the man and continued standing in line. Russell didn't know who the guys were, but he knew he wasn't gonna let them punk him out of his place in line. The moment muthafuckas thought you were a punk, they would keep picking on you, and Russell knew jail was the last place he was going to show a soft side.

"Nigga, do you hear me talking to you? I see you need to learn the rules, and you gonna fuck around and have to learn the hard way," one of the men said.

"Nah, Wayne, let me get his ass. I hear he like selling lil girls and you know how I feel about that," another one of the crew said, walking up and stepping to Russell.

Russell knew he didn't have many options. The man was too close in his personal space for Russell's comfort, and the rest of his crew had him surrounded. With nowhere to turn, Russell knew he would have to fight his way out of this, but he also knew he was outnumbered. Using all the strength he had, Russell punched the closest man to him, sending him falling back onto the tiled floor. Just like clockwork, the other three men pounced on Russell, throwing punch after punch, stomping him so viciously that Russell could feel his ribs breaking.

Finally, Russell heard a guard yell for them to stop before sounding the alarm, alerting the other guards of the fight. By the time the fight was broken up, Russell was a bloody mess and still wasn't able to reach out to Fatbar for his help.

"What y'all think about her?" Feez asked the crew as he watched Nikki walk to the bathroom.

"She seems cool, but where did she come from? We ain't never brought no random ass people into the crew and, now, you just bring her to one of our meetings? We can't even talk freely because she'd an outsider," Demo stated, feeling iffy about Nikki's presents.

"I just met her, but she cool as hell and it's something about her that I like. She solid, and I vouch for her. Just chill out and get to know her," Feez responded.

There was nothing normal about anyone in the crew bringing in outsiders. In their line of work, no new friends was the motto and it had worked thus far. They had all known each other since elementary school. Shayla was the newest member in the crew and she had even known them since middle school. However, Feez saw something in Nikki that would deem to be very lucrative for their business.

"Is she gonna be able to get down the way we get down?" Poncho asked, picking a shot glass up from the table and downing it.

"She's down to get money, I know that for a fact. The first day I meant Jania, she was trying to make some money. We need a fresh face in the group. Even if she don't do what we do, she can still help us get money. She 'bout it, just give her a chance y'all," Feez responded.

"Shit, we need another female in the crew. I'm sick of being the only bitch around all y'all niggas. If you say she good Feez, then she good. Matter fact, I'm about to go to the bathroom and have a lil girl chat with her," Shayla stated, standing to go find Nikki.

"Or what about that bitch that jumped the line? Her ass wasn't even that cute and her outfit was old as fuck. Cardi was taking picks on IG in that shit like two years ago," Cupcake said as she walked to the sink to wash her hands.

Nikki stood in the stall listening to everything the hating ass girl said, knowing she was talking about her. She knew she'd bruised the girl's ego with what she said in front of all the club goers that were in line; however, Nikki didn't care.

She was tired of people thinking they could treat her like she was nothing. Nikki was something and she was gonna carve out her place in this world if it killed her. Any other time, Nikki wouldn't have said anything to the girl; however, Cupcake had caught Nikki at the right time if smoke was what she wanted.

"Right, and her makeup wasn't even blended correctly. She looks like one of them tired ass bitches on her way to audition for a Zeus show. That hoe in here looking like the bride of Frankenstein. She needs to take her ass to Sephora for a damn color match," Peanut laughed.

"I know that's right!" Cupcake yelled, busting out into laughter and holding up her hand to slap five with Peanut.

Nikki's blood boiled as she listened to every word. *All this shit she talking when that hoe was quiet as fuck in my face,* Nikki thought. Nikki didn't know if it was her hormones from her pregnancy or if she was just tired of people but, either way, she'd had enough. Nikki busted out the stall heading directly to Cupcake. Cupcake didn't even have time to react before Nikki slapped fire to her, sending her hitting the tiled floor. Peanut, being quick on her feet, cocked her fist back and busted Nikki in her head, almost sending her to the floor.

"Bitch, get yo hands off my sista, fuck you think this is?" Peanut yelled before punching at Nikki again. This time, Nikki ducked and swung, busting two of her knuckles on Peanut's teeth.

She didn't stop there. Nikki grabbed Peanut by her fake

Brazilian bundles and laid punch after punch, hitting her in both the face and head, not letting up until she felt her hair being damn near ripped out of her head. Nikki had placed her tracks in securely; however, the way Cupcake was pulling on them, she knew they had to be on their last leg.

Still gripping Peanut's hair around her hand tightly, Nikki swung around and punched Cupcake with the other hand. Just then, Shayla walked into the bathroom and immediately grabbed her gun from her purse once she saw the two girls fighting Nikki.

"Get the fuck off her before both of y'all brains be all over this fuckin' bathroom!"

Cupcake, seeing the gun and not wanting smoke with Shayla, backed up, holding up her hands in surrender. Nikki still had a handful of Peanut's hair, so she couldn't go anywhere, even after she saw her sister throw in the towel.

"Jania, you okay girl?" Shayla asked, still holding her gun on Cupcake.

"Yeah, I'm good. These bitches ain't bout shit."

"Shayla, I'm sorry, no disrespect. I didn't know she was with you. She came out swinging on us. Me and my sista was just defending ourselves, that's it," Cupcake pleaded.

Nikki could see the fear in her eyes, and it made her chuckle. She wasn't talking tough anymore. The loud talking bitch was gone and replaced with a bitch that was shaking so frantically, Nikki thought she would piss herself. In one swift motion, Nikki swung Peanut around and let go of her hair, causing her to hit the floor.

"Look, bitch, I don't know what the fuck is going on, but Jania here is part of the crew. You know what the consequences are for fucking with the crew, right?" Shayla asked both girls while looking directly at Cupcake.

"I do, but I didn't know she was with y'all. You gotta know I would have never stepped to her like that if I would have known she was one of y'all. I ain't never seen her before tonight."

She knew Cupcake was telling the truth because she herself had just met her as well. However, none of that mattered. Feez had brought her around, so she was now part of the crew. That meant the same way Shayla was coming for her brothers was the same way she was going to come for Jania.

"I'll give you that and I'll let you slide but, from here on out, don't fuck with her. And let all them hoodrat ass bitches you be fuckin' with know that shit too. There won't be no conversation next time," Shayla stated, placing her gun back into her purse. "Now, get the fuck outta here," Shayla continued, watching the two girls scramble to pick up their purses and earrings from the floor before running out the bathroom.

Nikki walked to the mirror and ran her fingers through her hair several times in an effort to tame her now wild tresses. Nikki couldn't do anything but shake her head; she'd only been in Mississippi for a few days and she was already making enemies. She didn't give a damn, however; all she knew was that she was going to get her respect.

"Here girl," Shayla said, reaching into her purse and handing Nikki a brush.

"Damn, you got everything in there," Nikki joked.

"What the hell was that about?"

"Girl, they just some hating ass bitches. They was talking shit outside when they had to stand in line, and I didn't. Then, they were in here taking shit about me, so I had to say something. I ain't letting no bitch disrespect me and get away with it. So, I had to let them hoes know," Nikki informed.

"Well, you ain't got to worry bout them bitches no moe. Matta fact, now that you down with the crew, you ain't gonna have to worry 'bout nobody at all. We well known around these parts and got respect in these streets," Shayla responded.

"Who exactly is the crew? What do y'all do?" Nikki asked. She was still unaware what the crew did to make money and earn so much respect. However, she could tell by the way Cupcake and Peanut ran out the bathroom that they didn't want any smoke with Shayla.

"I'll leave it up to Feez to tell you all that. But I will tell you that the crew is a family, and we got each other's backs over everything. If you down with us, then you family too and we got you," Shayla said, smiling.

Nikki smiled back and thanked her, ready to talk to Feez and find out who 'the crew' really were. Once her hair was back in place, the pair walked out the bathroom heading back to the VIP section.

"Damn, I thought y'all got lost in there or something," Poncho said, as the two sat on the couch.

"Man, I'm glad I went to the bathroom when I did. Kimbo Slice ass was in there two-piecing Cupcake and her sista," Shayla informed, pouring herself a glass of champagne.

"What! Where them hoes at? Did you handle that shit Shay?" Feez asked while standing to his feet casing the club, looking for Cupcake and Peanut.

"Shit, I didn't have to, Jania was handling both they asses. She with the shits for real. She ain't gonna have no more problems out the two of them at all," Shayla replied.

"You good lil mama?" Feez asked, wrapping his arm around Nikki.

"Yeah, I'm straight. Them bitches ain't bout shit; I ain't even break a nail," Nikki stated.

"I made sure to tell them big mouth hoodrats that Jania was part of the crew now. You know them hoes gonna have word to the entire hood by tomorrow," Shayla laughed.

"You ain't lying about that shit. Them bitches is like the Shade Room of the hood," Demo chimed in.

"Nigga, I swear you ain't lying. Them bitches know everything that's going on before that shit even happens," Poncho laughed.

Nikki laughed right along with the rest of the crew, as they joked about the two sisters. Although she didn't know them and was still unsure what they did to make money, Nikki felt at home. She'd been around people her entire life that didn't make her feel as comfortable as the crew did. Shayla had said they were family and, for once, Nikki felt as though she belonged to a family.

"This is dope; I'm having a good time with y'all," Nikki stated. "However, I know you didn't just bring me here to dance and chit chat, so what's up? You said this was a money mission, I wanna know about that," she continued.

"Fasho, I got you. Imma give you a ride back to your hotel, so we can talk about it," Feez stated.

"Umm, I drove here," Nikki responded.

"It's all good. Poncho rode with me, so he can take your car and you can ride with me. It's too many ears in the club to be talking in here. I just wanted you to meet the crew. Now that they told me it's cool to bring you in, I can tell you what we about."

Nikki side-eyed Feez skeptically about leaving her car with Poncho. Her car was her only possession, the first thing she'd bought on her own so, to her, it was more of a rite of passage than a car. She couldn't see herself giving the keys to someone she really didn't know.

"Don't worry, Poncho gonna keep yo shit safe lil mama," Feez assured, noticing her hesitation.

Reluctantly, Nikki agreed and handed her keys to Poncho before letting him know the motel she was staying in. Feez said good bye to his crew before taking Nikki's hand and walking her out to his car. They walked side by side as he looked over at her and smiled.

"I don't know if I told you this, but you look amazing."

"Thank you, you look nice too and you smell really good," Nikki complimented.

Once they were in Feez's car and out of the parking lot, Feez was ready to answer all of her questions and see if she was down to join the crew.

"So, what's up, what do you and the crew do? Because I'm trying to make some money while I'm here in Mississippi," Nikki asked.

"We're assassins," Feez answered nonchalantly, keeping both his eyes on the road.

Nikki laughed so hard, she fell over and almost hit her head on the dashboard. She laughed for several seconds before she realized she was the only one laughing. Looking over at Feez, she saw he was still watching the road with a straight face. Her heart dropped when she realized he was serious.

"Wait, assassins, as in y'all kill people for money?" Nikki had to make sure she was hearing him correctly.

Out of all the things he could have said he did to make money, being an assassin was the last thing she thought of. She'd only killed one person in her life, and that was Cole, her child's father. However, could she just kill a random stranger just for a payout?

"Look, if you not down with it, that's cool, but say that shit now because once you part of the crew, ain't no leaving the game until we all ready to get out. We a team, and that's how we gonna move," Feez stated firmly.

He wanted to give her the choice while also wanting her to know that whatever she chose, her decision would be final. He wanted her down with his crew but wanted to make sure that 'crew' life was what she wanted. There was no second-guessing or half-stepping when it came to crew life; it was all or nothing.

Nikki thought for a minute; she could say no, find a job and get settled in California the way she'd planned. She wanted to give her child a normal life; however, when she thought about it, what was a normal life? Was it normal for her to be on the run because she killed her child's father for beating on her? She knew the money she had wouldn't last forever, so she would have to find a job. *Was it normal to have to work hours on end? Missing valuable time with your child while a daycare or nanny raise your child? What was really a normal life?* Nikki asked herself.

"How safe is this shit? If y'all out here killin' people, what's stoppin' people from killin' y'all? Shit, or the police puttin' y'all in jail?" Nikki asked while turning to look at Feez, giving him her full attention.

"We what's stoppin' anyone from coming after us. We ain't doing this for fun; dis a blood spot and we reign supreme. Ain't nobody fuckin' with us because they can't fuck with us. Now, as far as the police go, we have a system that assures our freedom. However, you can only find that out if you down with the crew. We can't be letting outsiders know our moves," Feez replied.

"If I'm gonna be out here killing people, it ain't gonna be for no chump change. I know y'all out here getting money but, if I do this with y'all, what is my cut gonna look like?"

"The crew is a family, so we split everything equally, no exceptions. So, yo cut will be the same as everybody's," Feez stated.

Damn, splitting the money equally would be dope. I know they getting big money and I'm ready to do the same. I wanna be sitting in the club in five-thousand-dollar outfits too. Getting down with them would be the way to assure my baby has a wonderful life filled with all the things I never had, she thought.

Giving her unborn child the life he or she deserved was Nikki's only focus and, in her mind, being down with the crew was the fastest way to do so. Nikki contemplated telling Feez she was pregnant; however, she stopped herself, thinking that he might want to hold off on letting her work. Nikki needed all the money she could get as fast as she could get it so, for now, she would hide her pregnancy until she could no longer do so.

"I'm down, do I need to sign a contract or something?"

Now, it was Feez's turn to bust out laughing, causing Nikki to turn her nose up.

"What's so funny?" she asked.

"This the streets, lil mama; we don't do paper trails, yo word is good enough," he replied.

Once back at Nikki's hotel room, she invited Feez in, so he could run down the play. She had to admit she was nervous because she'd never so much as shot a gun before. The one person she did kill, she'd overdosed, and it was only because he was hurting her. Although her thoughts were conflicted and her morals were trying to take over, the money that she would make trumped all.

"We got a job in a few days, so you can start then. Until then, you gonna hang around Shayla so she can show you the ropes. Now, this job pays two hundred thousand that we are now gonna split six ways. The job is in Miami, and that's our top rule. We never shit where we sleep, so none of our jobs will ever be in Mississippi. We get in and out. We fly in that day, get the job done and be back home the very next day. The police never know who they looking for because we don't leave no trace of who we are. We always hide our appearance and Shayla can hack any camera system. They can't catch what they don't see," Feez explained.

"But, how do y'all know who y'all killing? Like, people tell y'all they want a person dead and y'all go kill them?" Nikki asked.

"Well, yeah, that's exactly how it works. We do everything on the dark web on a completely untraceable site. The entire thing is foolproof. Our clients call a number that's hooked up to the site. The number is attached to a phone in my house that can't be traced. They tell us the name and send pictures and other information through the website. Nothing can be traced back to us at all," Feez explained.

Nikki nodded her head, ready to dive right in with the crew. Her palms itched, and she knew she was about to start getting some real money. This was it, the pot of gold at the end of the rainbow. Everything she had been through was all so she could get to this exact moment. Nikki smiled at the fact that she would come out on top, even though everyone around her had tried to keep her at the bottom. It was her time to shine, and Nikki wanted to blind these bitches. That night when she got in bed, Nikki felt the best she'd ever felt. For the first time in her life, Nikki felt as though she could take on the entire world.

CHAPTER FIVE

"Nakia, oh, my God, I'm so sorry friend," Simone called out sympathetically as she outstretched her arms, running over to hug Nakia as soon as she walked into the door.

Nakia didn't say a word, just fell into Simone's arms and cried. She couldn't believe that her life was playing out the way it was. She had gone from the happiest time in her life to the most hurtful in just the blink of an eye. Nakia wished she could rewind the hands of time and do everything differently. Sad thing about life, however, there were no redoes. Death was the final stage of physical life, and Nakia couldn't do a thing about her brother's transition.

"Simone, Nakia and the kids good here, right? I got some shit to handle and I can't be worried about them too," Raphael asked. He already knew the answer; however, he still wanted to make sure things would be good.

"This my sista right here," Simone said, pointing at Nakia. "She always gonna be good when she's with me. You know you don't even gotta ask that silly shit."

"My bad Simone, I already know," Raphael apologized, throwing his hands up in surrender.

"I got her and the kids. You just go do what you need to do, so you can get back to your family," Simone replied.

"I know you do." Raphael nodded before turning to walk away. He was still very much hurt by the loss of his parents and still very much blamed Nakia for it happening. He knew she wasn't the one who actually pulled the trigger; however, it was Nakia's actions that caused someone else to do so.

Rosa followed close behind Raphael as he made his way to his car where Blue was waiting. He didn't know where to find Manny; however, they would hit every corner until he found him. Raphael wasn't going to rest until both Manny and Russell were both dead. He would not let his parents die in vain and, although he was upset with Nakia, he would indeed avenge Jalyn's death as well. He would make sure that Manny and Russell felt the same pain that everyone around him did.

"Where we headed?" Blue asked, pulling out of Simone's driveway.

"I know Manny sometimes be at the spot on Outer Drive; let's pull up there and see what's up," Rosa suggested.

Blue nodded in agreement, making a U-turn before getting

on the freeway. Blue had been riding with the family for years. Fatbar himself had taken Blue off the streets and under his wing at the young age of fifteen. He was the only father figure that Blue knew, and Fatbar indeed looked at Blue like a son. Fatbar taught Blue the game and made sure he was able to make his own money. So, Blue felt like he owed it to Fatbar to do all he could to assure Manny was no longer breathing.

"Here go the house right here," Rosa said after fifteen minutes of driving.

"Pull up right in the driveway Blue; I want this nigga to see me. I ain't hiding no hands," Raphael stated.

Blue did as he was asked before the three of them exited the car guns in hand, none of them giving a damn about any nosy neighbors seeing them. They were on a mission and that was the only thing on their minds. Raphael was the first one to the door, knocking on it hard like he was the police. As soon as the door swung open, Raphael upped his Mag, pointing it directly to the head of the young shooter that opened the door.

"Where the fuck is Manny at?" Raphael yelled as he stepped into the house.

"I don't —"

Whack!

Raphael hit the young shooter in the head with the butt of his gun before he could even finish his sentence. "Don't fuckin' lie to me; you know exactly where Manny is or at least how to find him. Now, if you don't want bullets to be the next thing hittin' you in the head, then you will get Manny here now!"

O'shay didn't know what to do as he held his head, trying to slow down the blood that was gushing from it. He honestly didn't know where Manny was; in fact, Manny hadn't been at the spot in weeks. O'shay had no clue what was going; however, he couldn't tell Raphael that knowing that would probably be the last thing he said.

"I'll call him," O'shay mumbled as he scrambled to stand to his feet.

O'shay was just about to grab his phone when another shooter who heard all the commotion came from the back of the house. Without waiting to see what was going on, he began firing shots. Raphael was the first to duck and shoot back; however, he missed his target, allowing the shooter to fire several more shots.

"Rosa, get down!" Blue called out as he fired shots back.

Pow! Pow! Pow!

Blue was ruthless with the gun and was not letting up as he let off shot after shot, sending the shooter falling to the ground where he stood. Turning to O'shay, Blue let the last bullet in his chamber travel through his head, killing him instantly.

"What the fuck was that?" Rosa asked as she stood to her feet. "Where the fuck did he come from? We need to make sure nobody else is in here because we don't need no more surprises," she continued.

"Imma check the house," Blue stated before walking off.

He wanted to assure everything was safe before they did anything else. It would be just his luck that there was another shooter hiding in a room ready to take out all three of them. However, Blue wasn't having that. There would be no more bloodshed on their end if Blue had anything to do with it.

After checking the house and deeming it safe for everyone else, he went back to the front of the house where Raphael and Rosa were still waiting. He saw Raphael placing the dead shooter's finger to his phone.

"Yo, what you doing?" Blue asked.

"I'm going through his text messages, maybe Manny gave him is location in one of them," Raphael responded.

"That's the thing, he don't want to be found; he just wants to hunt us down. So, we have to figure out a way to get him to us and, then, we kill him," Rosa suggested.

"Yo, she got a point. We have to figure out a way to bring him to us. That way we know exactly where he is and when he's gonna be there," Blue agreed.

"Yeah, that's cool and shit, but how we gonna let him know where we gonna be if we can't contact him?" Raphael asked.

"Just let me think on it a little, Imma figure something out," Rosa stated.

~

"Mommy, did something happen to Uncle Jalyn?" Lexi asked as she entered the living room.

Nakia was sitting on the couch when Lexi walked in and sat right beside her, hugging her mother as if she could feel her pain. Nakia tried so hard to be strong in front of her daughter but, as soon as Lexi wrapped her tiny arms around her, she broke. Having to tell her sweet babies that their beloved uncle had passed away were words that she never wanted to speak.

"Uncle Jay is with God now, just like daddy," Nakia spoke through her tears.

Her kids were no stranger to death, having lost their father at such a young age. However, Nakia knew that the loss of their uncle would hit differently with them being a little older. She wished she could rewind the hands of time and go back to the moment she walked out the house to chase after Raphael. If only she had listened to Jalyn in the first place, none of this would have happened. He told her not to get involved in the situation at her job, but she didn't listen and called the police. He told her not to go outside and to get her things and go back to his place, but she didn't listen and ran outside. Even then, Jalyn ran outside with her and told her to come back into the house. However, she didn't listen, and he was shot. He'd told her and told her and, yet and still, she didn't listen.

"It's gonna be okay mama. Uncle Jay is still here," Lexi said softly.

"No, he's not, he's never coming back," Nakia cried. She

tried to wipe her tears as they fell, but they moved like waterfalls as they ran down her cheeks.

"Yes, he is. You told us when daddy died that he was now an angel and would watch over us and make sure we were safe. You told us that if we talked to him, he could still hear us. And you said that when we dream about him, that was him visiting us. You remember that mommy?" Lexi asked.

"Yes, I remember baby."

"So, if we could do that with daddy and Uncle Jay is there with daddy, then we can do the same with Uncle Jay," Lexi assured.

Look at my sweet baby. I'm the one that's supposed to be strong for her and she in here gettin' me together, Nakia thought as she smiled at Lexi. Hugging her tightly, Nakia kissed her forehead and thanked her. Even at seven years old, her daughter was wise beyond her years.

Rashaud walked in the living room with red swollen eyes, and Nakia knew Simone had told him the news. She opened her arms, and Rashaud ran to her sobbing loudly. Her heart ached for her son because she knew he would take the news the hardest. That night, Nakia sat with her children all night crying and laughing at memories of Jalyn.

CHAPTER SIX

Shayla picked Nikki up bright and early from her hotel room and took her to the gun range. Feez had told her she would have to learn a few things before she went on her first mission with them. With it only being a few days away, Nikki only had a short amount of time to learn all the skills she would need in order to keep herself and the crew safe. Shayla spent hours teaching Nikki how to shoot and reload. Shayla had already told Nikki they would stay there as long as it took for her to learn how to shoot her target and be able to change the magazine in under thirty seconds.

After over six hours of practice, Nikki finally had it down packed, sending an entire clip of nothing but head shots into her target. She was now able to change the magazine and empty the chamber in twenty seconds, and Shayla couldn't have been prouder. She felt like a proud mother whose child was walking across the stage at graduation.

"Okay, bitch, learning to shoot is just us scratching the surface; now, you gotta learn how to work these niggas. As the females of the crew, we sometimes have to lure these niggas somewhere so that the rest of the crew can get them," Shayla informed.

Nikki smiled, knowing she had that part in the bag. If it was one thing she knew how to do, it was to seduce a dude. Russell had taught her the art of that, and Nikki had perfected it. *Maybe this won't be so bad after all. I know they getting money, big money, and that's exactly what I need,* Nikki thought to herself.

"Come in Jania, we gotta go to the mall and pick you up a few wigs and outfits. It's very important that we conceal our identities the entire mission. Especially when were out in the open," Shayla informed, grabbing her purse and heading to her car with Nikki right beside her.

When they got to the mall, Shayla handed Nikki a stack of bills totaling ten thousand dollars and told her to buy everything she would need for the mission. Nikki's eyes widened as she took the money and placed in inside her purse. *Damn, I could get used to this,* Nikki thought as the pair walked into the mall.

Once they were done shopping, they were both tired and ready to go chill for the night. Shayla dropped Nikki back off at her hotel, telling her she would be back the following morning. They needed to study their vic, check his social medias and find out the places he frequented. You could tell a lot about a person by what they posted on social media so that was always the first place Shayla looked when studying a vic.

"Damn, that nigga fine as hell, you sure we gotta kill his sexy ass?" Nikki joked.

"And that's another thing Jania, you can't be getting attached to the vics. We got one job and that's to follow through with the mission. I don't give a fuck how fine, nice, or sweet a vic is, if we there for him, then he a dead man walking. Don't let yo fuckin' feelings get the entire crew fucked up," Shayla warned.

"I was just joking. I know the job and I'm not gonna fuck it up," Nikki confirmed. Nikki heard a knock at the door and got up to go look in the peephole.

"That gotta be Feez, he said he would stop by to make sure you had everything down packed," Shayla announced.

Nikki opened the door and allowed Feez entry to her room. His cologne invaded her nostrils as he walked past her, causing her pussy to moisten. It was one thing for a man to look good, but for him to smell even better than he looked had Nikki on ten. *Damn bitch, get it together. You here to make money, not find a man.*

"Y'all got yo shit all ready to go? We leave for Miami day after tomorrow. So, Jania, I hope you ready for yo first mission," Feez informed.

"Yeah, I'm ready. Shayla made sure I had everything down packed."

"Ok cool. This nigga Remo is 'That Nigga' in Miami and always has a ton of security around him. Now, we know the job pays, but this nigga always has stacks of cash on him that we can keep too. On top of all the jewelry he's always rocking. So, we have the chance to get an even bigger payout than the job pays," Feez stated.

"Do y'all ever know why these people are hiring y'all to take out these vics? Like, what did Remo do for someone to want him dead?" Nikki asked, genuinely wanting to know the answer.

She knew to them it was only a job; however, it was an odd job to have. She wondered if their conscience ever took over and it was hard to take a life. Or were they such horrible people that they didn't deserve to be on earth?

"It's not our business what these people do or have done. We have one job and that's to take them out. Only people we give a fuck about are the ones in our crew. Anyone else is fair game," Feez announced. "You not having second thoughts, are you?" Feez asked.

"Hell nah, I'm with the shits. I was just asking," Nikki replied.

"Good, because it's too late for any second thoughts. You a part of the crew and ain't no out unless we all agree," Feez reiterated.

TIANNA LAID naked across her bed as the cool air from the AC blew all over her body. She was full from eating her plate of leftovers from the dinner Tiny prepared the night before. She planned to chill and watch a movie before it was time for her to start work. She'd just turned on Netflix when Tiny knocked on her door.

"Come in!" Tianna called out.

"So, bitch, yesterday when I went to the grocery store, my Uber driver was trying to talk to me. He was some old ass white man, and I mean he was laying it on thick as fuck. So, you know me, I gave him one of our cards. Cuz, shit, ain't no way I'm doing anything with these niggas out here without gettin' paid for it. I ain't lookin' for no new friends. I gotta focus on getting my shit together for my baby. Hell, Imma need a few months off once I get big, so I gotta stack my shit now," Tiny informed.

"Yeah, I feel you on that shit," Tianna replied.

"Anyway, he just hit me up wanting to spend some money. I told him I didn't work alone and this muthafucka said he would take us both. He said he would pay us fifteen hundred a piece if we gave him a night he wouldn't forget. So, bitch, get dressed; he gonna be here in an hour. I figure if he comes now, we can give him a couple hours of attention before we start working for the night."

"Damn bitch, fifteen a piece for just a couple hours? That's easy ass money. And, for that, we can definitely give him a night he will remember his entire life. Shit, let me get sexy right quick," Tianna joked while getting on all fours, twerking her plump behind as she looked back at it.

"I know that's right bitch," Tiny laughed as well, playfully slapping Tianna's ass while sticking out her tongue.

Exactly an hour later, they were both looking good and smelling even better as they sat on the couch and waited for their client to arrive. Just like clockwork, the doorbell rang, alerting them that he was there. Tiny went and opened the door and allowed him access to the inside of their home.

"Well, hello handsome," Tiny greeted.

"It's so nice to see you again," he replied, smiling as he looked down at Tiny. He couldn't wait to have his way with her, and his manhood stiffened as he thought about the things he would do to her.

"It's nice to see you too, follow me. My homegirl is in the living room waiting on you. We figured we can have a few drinks before we make your fantasies come true," Tiny announced.

"That sounds like a plan, just lead the way, beautiful."

Tiny grabbed his hand, and the two walked into the living room where Tianna was sitting. Her eyes widened when Tiny and their client walked into the room, and she stood up to greet him.

"Jason? OMG, what the hell are the odds?" Tianna asked as she walked up to him and hugged him.

"You two know each other?" Tiny asked, confused as she looked from Jason to Tianna.

"Hell yeah, we do. Jason was my number one client when I broke away from Russell to start my own business. I used to see him at least three times a week. Shit, sometimes even more."

"Where the hell you been? I been looking for you for over a year. You still holding it down for Russell?" Jason said.

"Man, it's been a long year for me, and neither you or me have time for that story. As for Russell, I don't fuck with him no more. Me and my girl here started our own thing and it's been working for us. You still get girls from Russell?" Tianna sat back on the couch and poured a drink for Jason before handing it to him.

"I was for a minute after you went ghost on me, but then that nigga got caught up. Had the Feds all in his shit hard, and I didn't want to be a part of that shitshit, so I stopped fucking with him," Jason informed.

Tianna couldn't believe what she was hearing. She'd always thought Russell's shit was airtight. So, to hear he'd been caught up by the Feds had her in shock. "Damn, the Feds? That's fucked up, I didn't even know that shit was going on."

Tianna wasn't going to act like she felt bad for him because she knew he deserved everything he was getting now. She'd begged him not sell her to the Albanians. She kicked, screamed, and pleaded with him, but it all fell on deaf ears.

Now, Russell was getting his karma and Tianna was here for it.

"Yeah, his trial starts sometime this week. I might go for a few days just to show my support. It's hard to be behind bars and it's even harder when you got nobody on the outside to be there for you. I did ten years, so I know," Jason responded.

"Damn, I didn't know you did prison time," Tianna stated.

"Yep, before I started my own business and driving Lyft on the side, I was a young punk too. Got caught up with the wrong crowd and ended up getting into trouble. Spent ten years of my life paying for my stupid decisions, so I know exactly what Russell is going through."

"Yeah, I guess you do. It's a criminal case, so his trial gonna be downtown, right?" Tianna asked.

"Yep, at 36th District," he replied.

"Alright nah, it's enough of all that, we got shit to do. Don't be coming with this sad shit. We got fantasies to turn into reality," Tiny interrupted.

"Yeah, you right about that. Fuck that nigga Russell," Tianna said before taking a shot and unbuckling Jason's pants. Dropping to her knees, she took his manhood into her mouth. They spent the next two hours doing whatever Jason wanted to do and, when it was over, he handed Tianna and Tiny their money before leaving their home.

CHAPTER SEVEN

It was the day before the trial was set to start, and Russell had to admit he was a bit nervous. He'd been in the hole for the past twenty-four hours and had yet to contact Fatbar. With him not taking the plea deal the prosecutor was offering, he knew his case would go to trial; however, he hadn't been nervous until now. It was something about him not being able to call Fatbar that had him on edge. At least if Fatbar was able to reassure him that the witnesses wouldn't be able to testify, he would feel better. However, with him being in the hole, he was unable to make any phone calls.

Russell couldn't even call Travis and tell him to relay Fatbar a message. Last time he saw his brother, he was bussing him over the head with his gun, so Russell knew

Travis doing anything for him at this point was out of the question. Hell, for all he knew, Travis had flipped and was now working with the police.

His mind was running rampant, and Russell knew the only way to settle it was to know for sure he would get off. His lawyer was telling him to take the plea, letting Russell know that taking the case to trial would be deemed hazardous for him. However, Russell knew that if the witnesses were gone, then the police would have nothing, but were they really gone? Russell had no clue. The only way of knowing that was to get in touch with Fatbar, but that was out. So, Russell would be left with a wondering mind until the trial was over and he saw the outcome. In reality, Russell didn't know what he would do if Fatbar was unable to kill the witnesses and they indeed came to testify. He could only hope that Fatbar had indeed did his job and deaded the witnesses.

"Maybe the police haven't found the bodies yet, that's why they names still on the witness list," Russell said aloud to himself, trying to think positive.

Russell sat on the floor of his cell with his back against the wall. He hated not being in control of anything, but not being in control of his own life had Russell going crazy. He was so confident just a few hours before, thinking he was untouchable and that everything would work out in his favor. However, the closer it got to Monday, the more nervous Russell became. *Shit, even if them witnesses are dead, they still would have*

Deja and her girls, which is a whole fucking task force. They were the law and, one thing about it, the law gonna stick together. My lawyer better do his fucking job right or he gonna be the next person I have Fatbar take out for me, Russell thought.

Russell watched as a guard slid a tray of food through the door. Grabbing the tray, he looked down at it and scoffed at the slop they called dinner. Russell took the juice off the tray and drunk it before placing the tray onto the floor. *Ain't no way I'm eatin' that nasty ass shit, they got me fucked up. I gotta get the fuck outta here, this shit ain't gonna work for me.* Russell laid across his cot staring at the wall, praying that his trial went in his favor.

NAKIA WOKE up the next morning hoping that everything had been one awful dream. However, the moment she opened her eyes and realized she was in one of Simone's guest rooms, she knew it had really happened. Jalyn was gone and not coming back. Although she didn't want to, Nakia, being the only family he had, would be forced to start funeral arrangements for her baby brother.

"Damn, this shit is so fucked up," Nakia said out loud.

Nakia got out of bed and went to brush her teeth and wash her face. No matter how much she was hurting and wanting to stay in bed, she knew her children needed her more. Walking out the room, she smelled food cooking and headed down-stairs. Both Rashaud and Lexi were sitting in the couch watching cartoon, and Aden was lying in a pack-n-play while Simone cooked.

"Well, good morning beautiful. You want some coffee; I got that caramel creamer you like?" Simone greeted, seeing Nakia walk into the room.

Lexi and Rashaud both raised their little heads up from the couch and smiled when they saw their mother come into the living room. Rashaud jumped up from the couch and ran to hug Nakia. Her babies were hurt, and that broke her heart even more.

"Morning baby," Nakia whispered as she hugged Rashaud tightly. There was nothing good about this morning, so she left that word out.

"Morning Simone; yeah, I'll take some coffee," Nakia replied.

Lexi was the next to hug Nakia, grabbing her so tightly that Nakia could feel the love penetrating through her. She smiled at her precious baby girl because Nakia knew no matter how much Lexi was hurting, her first concern was making sure Nakia was alright.

"I love you, mommy," she whispered.

"I love you too, baby."

Nakia walked over to the pack-n-play and picked up Aden before walking over to Simone's kitchen island. She took a seat on one of the stools and rocked Aden in her arms. Simone placed a cup of coffee and the creamer in front of her.

"Thank you," Nakia said

"You're welcome. I didn't know what you would want to eat, so I just made all your favorites. We got eggs, waffles, fruit, fried chicken, bacon, crab legs, shrimp, sausage, grits, and bitch some Krispy Kreme doughnuts," Simone declared.

Nakia could tell Simone was trying to be in good spirits for their sake; however, she could also tell by the amount of cooking she was doing that she was just as much in shambles as they were.

"Friend, you did not have to cook all this; the kids would have been fine with a bowl of cereal," Nakia stated.

"Yes, I did. Staying busy is my way of coping with what's going on. So, bitch, do you want me to make you a plate or nah? Cuz me and the kids 'bout to eat!" Simone said, waving a cooking spoon in the air.

"Gone on head and make my plate sis," Nakia responded, feeling her stomach growl at the smell of the delicious food.

Simone chuckled, made the kids' plates and sat them down at the table before tending to Nakia. Knowing Nakia hated her food to touch each other and wanting to give her a bit of everything, Simone pulled two plates and two bowls from the cabinet and began scooping food onto them. She placed the two bowls, one filled with grits and the other filled with butter, in front of her before giving her the other plates.

"Here friend, let me take the baby so you can eat," Simone offered.

Nakia handed Aden to her before digging right into her food. After going a day without eating, Nakia didn't know just how hungry she was until the food was right in front of her. After pouring hot sauce and honey over her chicken and cracking open a few crab legs, Nakia could feel the nourishment coming back to her body.

"I think Imma go over to Jay's apartment today. I wanna look threw his closet and get his size. I'm gonna have to buy some clothes to bury him in," Nakia stated sadly.

"Nah, friend, you don't gotta do that. I'll go get his size for you. It's too soon for you to be doing all that," Simone informed.

She knew her friend was hurt and didn't know if her being in Jalyn's space so soon would be a good idea for her. The last thing Simone needed was for Nakia to be triggered and do something to hurt herself. She didn't thing Nakia would do anything to harm herself; however, you never knew what people would do when they were hurt. When she lost her children's father, Simone though Nakia would never be happy again, but this was her brother. So, Simone vowed to do whatever she could to assure Nakia didn't slip back into depression.

"Nah, I got it. I think it would make me feel a bit better to be around his things. I'm gonna eventually have to pack them up anyway. He was renting his apartment, so you know how that go," Nakia replied.

Simone just nodded her head. She didn't want to push her too much and, if Nakia thought it was a good idea, then she would step back.

"Can I come with you?" Rashaud asked, walking up to Nakia.

"Sure, you can come. You wanna come too, Lexi?"

"Yep," Lexi replied.

Once Nakia was finished eating, she went to get dressed. Her thoughts were all over the place and she wondered what would come out of this. Would Raphael get justice for Jalyn and his parents by killing Manny? Would Manny come back and kill her first before Raphael got to him? Or was Raphael the enemy all along and he was the one that started it all? *Damn Jay, why didn't I just listen to you?*

Nakia didn't know who to trust but, at that moment, she vowed to herself and her brother that she would get to the bottom of this, getting justice for him if that was the last thing she did. She was also gonna find out exactly who Raphael was because it was clear to her that he wasn't the man she thought he was. *I'll be damn if I continue to sleep with the enemy.*

After getting dressed, she and the kids piled in the car and headed to Jalyn's apartment. Rashaud and Jalyn bonded over video games, so she would be sure to let Rashaud pick all the games he wanted before Nakia donated the rest. She just wanted to be around his things, so she would be closer to him. To smell his cologne so she would never be able to forget what he smelled like. She missed her brother tremendously and it had only been two days. Nakia didn't know how she would make it through the rest of her life without him. Jalyn was the best brother anyone could have asked for and, although Nakia was indeed sad, she was happy that God had loaned him to her for the time he did.

CHAPTER EIGHT

Manny sat outside watching Nakia and her kids while they walked into the apartment building. He wasn't aware of who stayed there, but he was going to sit outside until he found out. Manny had switched cars since the shooting at Nakia's house. He didn't expect for the police to be there but, since they were, he knew they at least had a description of his car. He didn't need the police catching him before he was at least able to complete his mission. So, he was going to have to stay two steps ahead of them.

It was pure luck that had him see Nakia at the red light, and he quickly made a U-turn and followed her to her destination. He was hoping that Nakia would lead him to Raphael because he still had some unfinished business to handle. Even though he wanted to kill Nakia as well, he knew he had to be wait until he had eyes on Raphael. He thought it was him standing outside with Nakia that day. However, after watching the news, he'd learned that he'd shot Nakia's brother. It would make his lifetime if he could kill both Raphael and Nakia together the way he did Fatbar and Harlin.

Once he'd killed them, he would have gotten the justice Niko deserved, and that was all Manny wanted. Once that was done, he would leave Michigan and never look back. He had no family left, so it was easy for him to just pick up and leave. The hardest part was the fact that his only brother wasn't with him. They'd done everything together for as long as Manny could remember but, now, it had been all taken away from him by the same family that said they loved them.

"You 'bout to join Fatbar and Harlin in hell real soon," Manny said out loud, speaking to Nakia while knowing she couldn't hear him.

Manny didn't have a plan other than to kill everyone who was involved. He tried not to be sloppy and leave anything behind for the police to find. He already knew they were looking for him, so he had to be sure not to leave anything around that would lead them to him. The last thing he wanted was for the law to catch up to him before he was able to get to everyone. He'd almost been caught when he tried to kill Nakia outside their home. An unmarked police car pulled up out of nowhere and began firing shots at him. He was lucky to get away and, although he didn't kill Nakia, he had definitely killed her brother. So, now, at least he knew she was hurt just like he was.

"What up doe?" Manny answered his ringing phone that snapped him out of his thoughts.

"Yooo, Manny, you need to get over to the Outer Drive spot. Some shit popped off and everybody in here dead. Nigga, it's blood everywhere!" Javon yelled into the phone.

"What? Everyone like who? Who was all there?" Manny spoke frantically into the phone. The thought of him being robbed had Manny seeing red. He needed to get there and see just how much money and work was taken from him. He was gonna need all his funds to leave Michigan, so whoever had robbed him was definitely dying tonight.

After letting Javon know he was on the way, Manny pulled from in front of Jalyn's apartment and sped down the street. *You got lucky today, Raphael, both you and yo bitch get to live another day,* Manny thought. He couldn't believe someone had robbed him. Out of all the things that could have happened, this was the last thing he needed. This robbery might indeed set Manny back tremendously. Manny was going to need all his savings to get out of Michigan after completing his mission. Now, he would have to hustle even harder.

Doing a hundred on Southfield, Manny pulled up to his spot within fifteen minutes. Jumping out of his car and damn near running to the door, Manny was taken aback at the crime scene he'd walked into. The boys he had in the spot were laid out with holes throughout their bodies. Manny couldn't believe his eyes as looked around at the bullet-ridden walls.

"Yo, who the fuck hit us? Have you looked around and counted up how much they took yet?" Manny asked Javon.

"That's the thing, I looked, and everything is still here. They didn't take the money or the work," Javon informed.

Manny instantly knew exactly what this was. This was no robbery; this was Raphael trying to make a statement. It was a war, and Manny was ready to stand on the front line. His so-called family had been involved with the murder of his only brother. So, he had no choice but to retaliate by any means necessary. It was an eye for an eye.

"This was Raphael," Manny whispered.

"Raphael? You talking 'bout yo cousin Raphael? Why would this be him?" Javon asked, confused about what Manny was telling him. Javon knew this business Raphael was in and couldn't see him coming to Manny's spot shooting anything or anybody.

"It's a long ass story, but I'm telling you it's him and I'm gonna get this nigga!"

"O'shay was the lil homie. Whoever did this to him gotta be dealt with. If it was Raphael, then so be it. I'm ridin' out for the homie, just like I know he would do for me," Javon stated.

Javon had no ties to the war between Raphael and Manny. He didn't even know it existed until he'd walked into the spot that day. However, the moment Raphael put bullets into O'shay, it put Javon in the middle of their war. *If Raphael put bullets in O'shay, then he had to feel his bullets too,* Javon thought. O'shay was a good kid, had just started living life. He was only nineteen, and Raphael had ended his life over something he knew nothing about.

"Where do we find Raphael?" Javon asked. He was ready for the shits and, if a war was what Raphael wanted, then Javon was about to bring one to him.

"I don't know yet but, when you called, I was watching his bitch at some apartment building. I don't know whose apartment it was, but I got the address. I'm sure she will go back there and, when she does, we can let her lead us right to Raphael," Manny revealed.

"Yeah, let's do that shit cuz this nigga gonna feel this hollow tips."

"Do me a favor and call Big L to come and clean this shit up and call their families to let them know we are sorry for their losses and that we will cover all funeral expenses," Manny stated before walking out the door.

CHAPTER NINE

*B*ailey stood in her mirror trying to apply her makeup. Her hands shook so badly that she opted out of using eyeliner out of fear of poking herself in the eyes. She was nervous about the trial and didn't want to testify. In fact, she and Nakia had vowed to each other that they simply would not do it. However, when Agent Scott told her the trial had been moved up and threatened her with prison time if she did not show up to testify, she figured it would be in her best interest if she just went and got it over with.

With only about fifteen minutes before the car was coming to pick her up, Bailey wished she could just change her mind and not go. Her palms were sweaty and, no matter what she did, she couldn't stop shaking. Her nerves were clearly getting the best of her, and Bailey wished she could rewind time. If she could, she would have never told the police anything.

Although she felt good about getting those girls to safety, she had now put herself in harm's way.

The doorbell rang, and Bailey's heart dropped to her stomach. She took a few deep breaths before grabbing her purse and walking to the door. "You got this Bailey, just get it over with so you can be done with it," she told herself out loud before opening the door.

"Hello, my name is Officer Gomez and I'll be your escort to court today. If you are ready to go, then we can be on our way."

Bailey nodded her head before closing and locking her door behind her. This was it, and there was no turning back now. Bailey only prayed that she wouldn't be in this alone, and the thought of jail time had scared Nakia into testifying as well. She hadn't spoken with her in several weeks and, the last time they did, they had made a vow. If there was any time Bailey hoped Nakia went back on her word, this was it. *I hope I'm not making the wrong decision by testifying,* Bailey thought as the black unmarked car she was riding in drove down 94.

The thirty minutes it took for them to drive to the 36th District court went by way too fast for Bailey's liking. Before she knew it, she was being escorted through the building and into a small room where two other agents waited for her arrival.

"Good morning, Ms. Malone; I'm Special Agent Jones and that's my partner Special Agent Lafferty. We are here to walk you through some of the questions you may be asked on the stand," Agent Jones informed.

She was a light skinned younger woman, probably in her mid-twenties. She had curly hair she'd placed neatly into a low ponytail. She wore a dark gray pants suit with a black shirt underneath. She'd applied light makeup to her face which gave her a natural look, and Bailey thought she was beautiful. So much so that Bailey thought she was much too beautiful to have such a dangerous job. Agent Lafferty was a white woman with straight red hair that she also placed in a low ponytail; however, she had a part down the middle. Her thick unkempt eyebrows and dry wrinkled face showed Bailey that she didn't care as much about her appearance as Agent Jones did. If they were to play good cop bad cop, Agent Lafferty would definitely be the bad cop. She reminded Bailey of Miss Trunchbull from the movie Matilda. Bailey could see her in the courtroom now telling one of the witnesses to chop her pigtails off before court tomorrow or she would.

"Good morning, it's nice to meet you both," Bailey replied.

"You can have a seat and we will get started," Agent Lafferty stated, pointing to a chair.

Bailey smiled nervously before walking over to the chair and sitting down. She crossed her right leg over her left before nervously placing her foot back to the floor and placing her left leg over her right.

"Ms. Malone, you stated in your original statement to

police that you work at the Courtyard Marriott where the defendant stayed for several nights, correct?" Agent Lafferty asked, looking Bailey directly in her eyes.

"Yeah, that's where I work," Bailey answered.

"Ms. Malone, please remember that you answer each question with a yes or no answer. If the question prompts you to elaborate, then you do so after answering yes or no to the question."

"Yes, I work at the Courtyard Marriott," Bailey stated once more.

"Did you see the defendant there?"

"Yes, I did, several times," Bailey answered.

Bailey sat there for about forty-five minutes going over her initial statement several times. When they were finally done, Bailey asked the agents if Nakia showed up to court that day. It was the one question that had been on her mind all morning and she needed to know the answer.

"I'm not sure. The two of you have to stay separate, and we were only placed to be with you today," Agent Jones responded.

Bailey was even more nervous at that point seeing how no one she'd spoken with knew if Nakia was testifying or not. She wanted to call Nakia but had been prompted by the officers not to have any contact with each other once they entered the courthouse. Bailey was on edge and couldn't seem to calm herself down.

"I need to use the bathroom," Bailey informed the agents.

Special Agent Jones looked down at her watch before nodding her head and motioning Bailey to follow her. Walking her down the hall and to the closest bathroom, she let her know to return to the briefing room when she was finished. Bailey agreed and walked into the bathroom.

TIANNA DRESSED in a black pants suit with a black lace cami underneath. Her hair was flat-ironed bone straight with a middle part, and the red lipstick she wore was the only pop of color to her outfit. The large black hat she wore covered the top part of her face and was perfect for hiding her identity. Tianna didn't dress up much, she actually had never gotten the chance to. But here, she was dressed to the nines and looking good as hell.

"Damn, bitch, you lookin' fine. Where you off to so early in the damn morning?" Tiny asked.

"I'm on my way to court. That guy that Jason was telling us about the other night was the reason I was in Albania in the first place. I went through a lot because of that man, and I wanna see that muthafucka get exactly what he deserves," Tianna informed.

From the time she'd touched down in Albania, she'd been waiting for the day Russell received his karma, and that day had finally arrived. Tianna couldn't wait for Russell to see her face when she walked into his trial. She knew the judge would find him guilty, and she couldn't wait to laugh while he was being sent away, the same way he'd done to her.

"Are you sure this is what you want to do? This could open a lot of old wounds," Tiny asked.

She knew exactly how Tianna felt. She too had been a victim of sex trafficking, being sent to Albania by someone she thought loved her. However, now that she'd gotten out and started doing good on her own, she didn't know if she would want to relive past trauma the way Tianna was about to.

"This is something I have to do. I need to see him being locked away. I need to hear the judge tell him how many years he will be locked away for. And, I need for him to see my face before he gets put under the jail. This shit is for me, not him," Tianna revealed.

Tiny nodded her head in understanding, seeing everything from Tianna's point of view. Tiny offered to go with Tianna and be there in support of her; however, Tianna declined her offer, knowing this was something she needed to do alone. She continued to get dressed. Once she was finished, she looked like she was going to a funeral. She smiled at herself in the mirror, knowing she was dressed well for the occasion.

Surprisingly, Tianna wasn't nervous at all as she rode in the backseat of her Uber. She was no longer scared of Russell and wanted him to know that. After the year she'd spent in Albania and all the things she'd endured, there wasn't much that would scare her. So, Tianna was ready to face anything. She knew she had Russell to thank for that.

Tianna walked into the court room with her head held high as she took a seat in front where she knew Russell would see her. Tianna couldn't wait to see the look on Russell's face when he walked in and saw her sitting there.

RUSSELL WALKED down the long hallway in shackles being escorted by two armed guards. His heart raced and sweat poured from his head as he walked into the first day of the rest of his life. He didn't know what the day would bring and, for the first time in years, Russell wished he'd chosen a different career path. It was his love of money and his ability to manipulate both women and underage girls that had led him her. His lawyer had told him to take the plea, and Russell had refused. He was now rethinking that decision as well.

Russell walked into the courtroom and took a seat at the table next to Kyree. He didn't even look at any of the people that were present in the courtroom. They were all obsolete to him. His only focus were the people that would be in front of him and not behind him.

"You ready for this shit?" Kyree whispered, leaning over so only Russell could hear him.

"As ready as I'll ever be."

Russell's palms were moist and he wiped them on the pants of the suit Kyree had sent to him. He was ready to get to the end of the trial and hoped it didn't last too long. He was ready to hear the words *not guilty*, so he could get on with his life. He was ready to put all this behind him, so he could start his new life. Russell had promised God that if he got him out of this one, he would completely change his life.

"All rise, the Honorable Judge Greg Jackson presiding!" the bailiff yelled before everyone in the courtroom stood to their feet.

CHAPTER TEN

ikki couldn't believe how quickly the day of the mission came as she stepped onto the private jet. Nikki had never been on a private jet before, and she felt important as she took her seat. In her mind, a PJ was for the rich and famous, but here she was a regular chick from the hood flying like the upper echelon. *Damn, I can get used to this*, Nikki thought to herself as she looked out the window waiting for takeoff.

She had yet to tell the crew that she was pregnant and, although she didn't want to tell them, she knew they would find out eventually. So, she made the choice to tell them once the mission was finished.

"Alright, y'all, as we all know, this is Jania's first mission. Although Shayla has trained her on everything she needs to know, I still want everyone to look out for her!" Feez called out.

"You know we got her, that's how we get down. No homie left behind," Poncho stated.

"Right, you know you don't even have to tell us that shit," Demo reiterated.

Nikki smiled at the way her newly found family already had her back. Who would have thought that she would find so much love in Mississippi, after searching for it her entire life? Nikki was still a bit reluctant to actually kill someone; however, if that would assure her family, love and money, then she would do what she had to do.

"Okay, good. I already know but you know I had to make sure," Feez stated.

"Fuck all that, where the champagne at?" Regal asked, motioning the flight attendant over to him.

"We need champagne and six glasses," Regal stated.

"Umm, I'll just have some water," Nikki said.

The attendant nodded her head and went to go retrieve their order. Once she was back with the drinks, Regal poured the champagne into each glass and proceeded to make a toast.

"Here's to family, money and more money!" he yelled, as everyone raised their glasses and Nikki raised her water bottle.

"Alright y'all, get relaxed, get some sleep, do whatever you need to do while we fly because once we touch down, it's game time," Feez stated.

Nikki slept for most of the flight, feeling comfortable in the soft leather seats. By the time she opened her eyes, they were preparing for landing. It was at that point that Nikki became nervous. She was having second thoughts about going on the mission.

What if I fuck something up and get one of us hurt? What if I fuck something up and I get hurt? Or what if I fuck something up and we don't get paid?

A million and one what ifs ran through Nikki's brain as she and the crew stepped off the jet. She knew it was too late to turn back now. She'd been warned upon entry of the crew, there was no getting out. So, she knew she was stuck until they all decided otherwise. Nikki didn't know if it was the pregnancy or her nerves getting the best of her. However, before she knew it, she had thrown up right on the runway.

"Damn, sis, you good?" Shayla asked, coming to Nikki's aid.

"Yeah, I'm good, I think that flight got my stomach messed up."

Nikki rinsed her mouth out using the water bottle she'd been drinking from before popping a stick of gum in her mouth. The crew of six got into the black sprinter that was waiting for them and made their way to the Airbnb they had rented. Although they were only in town for one night, the crew always stayed in style. So, when they pulled up to the six-bedroom eight-bathroom home, nobody was impressed but Nikki.

"Damn, this house big as fuck and it got a pool too? I can't believe y'all got this big ass house for only one night," she stated.

"It don't matter if it's one day or one hour. We always roll like this," Feez informed. "You betta go pick out yo room before Shayla takes the good one," he continued.

"Too late, Demo already put our things in the master suite. But I did see a really nice room down the hall from mine. You can have that one, Jania."

Feez couldn't do anything but laugh at the way Shayla always though the master suite belonged to her and Demo. No matter whose turn it was to pay for the Airbnb, the master suite was always theirs.

"Jania, do me a favor. After you get settled in, I need you to gather everyone in the living room for a meeting. We only have a few hours before the mission begins, and I need to make sure everyone knows their posts," Feez informed.

"I got you, Feez," she replied before heading upstairs to find her room.

Nikki walked into her room and was in awe at the décor. The entire room was white and gold with hits of pink and rose-gold throughout. The plush king-sized bed was all white with pink and gold bedding. The room looked like it was fit for a queen, and this wasn't even the master bedroom. *Damn, I can't wait to see what Demo and Shayla's room looks like. If mine is this big, theirs gotta look like an apartment or some shit,* Nikki thought.

Making her way to her en-suite bathroom, Nikki got

undressed and took a shower. She hated to sweat, and the Miami heat had already begun to make her feel sticky. Once Nikki was clean and dressed, she gathered up the crew and they all met in the living room.

"Alright, y'all, we leaving here in about two hours, so I need to make sure everything is on point. We know Remo's gonna be at Club Wet tonight, so that's where we gonna be. We also know he's gonna be surrounded by his goons, so it's not gonna be easy to take him out. But that's where Jania and Shayla come in," Feez announced.

"What you mean?" Nikki asked, seemingly confused.

"One thing about a nigga is he loves pussy. That pussy got power in it. It will make muthafuckas lie, cheat, kill and steal. So, y'all gotta use that pussy power to get him away from the goons that's gonna be guarding him tonight."

"We can definitely do that shit, you know how I roll Feez," Shayla answered.

"Nah, tell me how you get down?" Demo joked. "Let me find out you letting anyone so much as smell my pussy, it's gonna be a fucking problem," he continued.

"Boy, shut up, this is work, not real life," Shayla informed, hitting Demo's arm playfully.

"Calm down Demo, you know Shayla ain't giving that pussy to nobody but you. I tried when we was teenagers and I still ain't got it yet. So, I know a rando ain't getting shit," Regal joked.

Everyone burst into laughter because they all knew

Regal's statement was true. Shayla only had eyes for Demo since the moment they got together.

"These are our new identities for the night. We all have one, just in case we have to show them for any reason," Feez announced as he handed each one of them a fake ID before they all retreated to their rooms.

Once everyone was dressed and strapped, they went out to the garage where the two black SUVs were parked. Shayla and Nikki got into one while Feez, Demo, Poncho and Regal got into the other. Shayla and Nikki were to go inside the club where Remo would be sitting in the VIP section. Their job was to get into his section and lure him out of it. Poncho and Regal would also be inside the club to scope out everything while Feez and Demo sat outside in the parking lot.

"Y'all ready?" Demo asked, hopping into the driver's seat of the SUV.

"Hell yeah, let's get this money!" Regal replied.

"Jania, you good?" Feez asked, walking over to Nikki and grabbing her hands.

He knew she had to be nervous with this being her first mission and wanted to make sure she was okay with everything going on. He wanted to make her feel as comfortable as possible because he didn't need her making any mistakes.

"I'm not gonna lie; I'm a little nervous, but I'll be okay. I promise you, I got this."

If it was one thing Nikki knew, it was how to make a man eat from the palm of her hand. If she had learned nothing else from Russell, it was that. Nikki had made a lot of money in the time she'd worked with Russell. Even though she didn't see the money, Nikki knew she was good at her job.

"I believe you," Feez stated before kissing Nikki on her forehead. "Y'all be safe," he continued.

"Damn, bitch, let me find out you Feez new thang," Shayla joked

Nikki was just as stunned as Shayla was. Feez was fine as hell, and Nikki was indeed attracted to him. However, she was unaware that he felt the same about her. That sweet forehead kiss had warmed both her heart and her love box. *Get it together bitch, you got another man's whole baby inside you. Now is not the time to be fallin' for no other niggas*, Nikki thought as she got into the passenger seat of the SUV.

The club was packed from wall to wall, and it took Nikki and Shayla a thirty-minute wait in line in order to get in. Once they were inside, they knew why. The entire club was made of glass, from the three dance floors to the walls and the balconies. The blue lights gave the effect of being surrounded by water. *Damn, now I see why they call it Club Wet,* Nikki thought.

Shayla and Nikki stayed close as they made their way to the bar. Neither one of them were going to drink. Nikki was pregnant, and they both needed to be on their A game. However, because they had to play a part for the mission, they were going to give the illusion they were drinking. They'd studied Remo enough to know that he picked out girls in the club to come to his section, and all they had to do was look good. Both Shayla and Nikki had went all out for that reason alone.

Nikki was dressed in a black Chanel mini-dress with a pair of black and gold YSL pumps. The old jewelry she wore was a nice added touch. Her makeup was beat for the gods and the thirty-inch blond bust-down lace frontal she had on laid perfectly on the top of her head. Shayla looked equally as good with Fendi from head to toe. Everything from her body-suit to her shoes to her jewelry were all Fendi while her long, curly red lace-front was full of body and hung past her ass. The two definitely stood out as two top bad bitches in the club.

After grabbing their glasses, which were filled with water and a twist of lemon, they sipped their drinks while doing a slight two-step to the music. The club was so packed, they had to scan it a few times in order to spot Regal and Poncho. Nikki felt a sense of relief once she spotted them ducked off at a table at the far end of the club. The table where they resided had a clear view of Remo's section, so they would be able to watch them once the ladies got inside.

"That nigga over there lookin' at us already," Shayla spoke. She'd already spotted Remo looking over in their direction a few times since they'd come in and she knew it wouldn't be long before he called them over to introduce himself.

"Well, we need to give him somethin' to really look at," Nikki responded.

Understanding the assignment, Shayla bent over and started twerking her plump ass to the music. Shayla was a beautiful woman, and everyone knew that. However, her biggest and best asset was her ass. She'd paid good money for the best doctors to sculpt her body to perfection. Shayla was definitely using it to her advantage tonight. Nikki quickly followed suit, sexy dancing right along with Shayla. Within minutes, they both spotted one of Remo's goons coming towards them. Shayla looked up at Nikki and gave her the *this is it* look.

"How you ladies doing tonight?" the goon asked loudly, so they could hear him over the music.

"We're good, how about yourself?" Nikki asked sexily.

"Good. My boss sent me over here to invite you ladies to his section."

Both Nikki and Shayla looked over in the direction the goon was pointing to like they hadn't come there for that exact reason. Shayla smiled, waiting to make eye contact with Remo before licking her lips. She nodded her head up and down at the goon to say yes before making her way over to his VIP section. Nikki quickly followed, swaying her hips and slightly hypnotizing the goon that was sent to summon them. The four women in the section rolled their eyes the moment the girls walked in, knowing that whatever they thought would happen with Remo tonight was deaded now that they were there. Nikki and Shayla were the two baddest bitches in the cub and the four women in VIP knew it.

"Good evening, ladies. I'm Remo and I'm glad y'all chose to join me. Grab a glass and have a seat. Let's get to know each other."

Shayla wasted no time squeezing her hips between Remo and the woman sitting closest to him. The woman rolled her eyes and jumped to her feet for what she thought would be a fight. However, before she could protest, one of Remo's goons grabbed her and escorted her out of his section.

"Really Remo? You gonna kick me out, so you can chill with some other bitches? Fuck you, nigga!" the woman yelled loud enough over the music that everyone around the section could hear her.

Shayla couldn't do anything but shake her head at the way this woman was acting. She knew the woman felt slighted; hell, she would too. This woman, however, was about to cause a scene in the club for nothing. Little did she know, Shayla was plotting to kill Remo, not fuck him.

"I been down for yo ass and you gonna play me? You fucked up this time, nigga," she continued.

"Boom, get this bitch away from my section and out this club," Remo informed another one of his goons.

Remo's word was all the goon needed to hear. Boom quickly walked over to the woman and picked her up, placed her over his shoulder and headed towards the door. The woman called Remo everything except a child of God as she was carried out the club. Nikki couldn't help but chuckle at the events as she watched the woman make a complete fool of herself.

"My bad 'bout that. I don't know what all that was about. It's good vibes only over here, and that bitch clearly wasn't a vibe," Remo apologized.

"It's all good, we not here for her anyway. We came to chill with you. I'm Angel and this is my girl Dominque," Shayla introduced, giving Remo the names on their fake ID's.

"Angel huh? Yeah, yo mama knew what she was doing when she named you. I ain't never seen y'all in Miami, and I run this city. Where y'all from?" Remo asked, pouring Deleon into his glass.

"We from Chicago, we just here trying to have some fun for a long weekend," Nikki replied.

The music dropped, and the DJ dropped another one. JT blasted through the speakers wanting to know what you workin' with, and the club went crazy.

"Awww shit, that's my muthafuckin' song!" Shayla yelled out as she stood to her feet and started dancing sexily in front of Remo. On cue, Nikki stood up and began dancing right with her.

The other girls in the section all knew it was over for them when Remo's eyes locked on Shayla and Nikki. His dick began to stiffen and he knew he would be taking the two of them home tonight. Two of the girls just got up and left, trying to save themselves the embarrassment of being sent away. However, one girl remained. Nikki noticed how she eyed

Shayla while rolling her eyes and knew she was jealous. So, with that, Nikki put on a show. She dropped down low, placing her face directly in front of Shayla's pussy. She licked out her tongue and moved it up and down to the same rhythm that she bounced her ass with. She knew they needed to get Remo alone, and she was prepared to pull out all her old tricks to make that happen. Her eyes were on dollars signs and nothing else. So, Nikki was going to make sure she executed the mission.

"Dayum!" Remo yelled out, ready to leave the club at that moment and take the two of them to a room. He could only imagine the type of fun he could have with the two of them. He sat there and watched them as though he was streaming a good ass movie.

"Nigga, I'm glad Demo ass ain't in here. He would have busted our shit all up seeing Jania on his bitch like that," Poncho joked.

Regal couldn't do anything but laugh knowing Poncho was telling the truth. Demo didn't play no games when it came to Shayla, so seeing Jania all over her like that would have made him blow their entire cover. Poncho and Regal watched, as Remo stood up and whispered into Shayla's ear. They knew shit was about to go down. Within a few minutes, Shayla and Nikki were walking out the club with Remo and his goons. Poncho shot a text to Feez, letting him know they were on the move before they walked out the club as well.

"Where yo room at? I'm ready to get into something right now," Shayla said sexily as she grabbed Remo's crotch.

"It's not too far; we going to the Hilton, that shit right down the street."

Hearing the location, Nikki quickly texted Feez, letting him know where they were going before anyone even noticed she had her phone out. The three of them got into the back seat of the SUV while the two goons got in the front. Once everyone was inside, they pulled out of the parking lot and headed to the hotel. Shayla and Nikki both knew this would be the only time they would have to seduce him enough to allow his goons to go home for the night.

"Damn, we bout to have some fun tonight, huh?" Remo asked, as Shayla and Nikki licked on both sides of his neck.

"Yeah, daddy, we tryin' to get loose," Shayla whispered.

"Yeah, that's what I like to hear," Remo replied, reaching over and grabbing a hand full of Shayla's ass.

They pulled up to the hotel within five minutes, and the two goons who drove them there got out the car. Nikki watched as they walked over to the car of goons behind them and said a few words before walking into the hotel.

"Are they gonna be with us the whole night? We here to fuck with you, not them," Nikki said.

"I don't go nowhere without my security, not even to get pussy. They won't be in the room with us, but they gonna be close," Remo responded

Neither Shayla nor Nikki liked that response, knowing that

would deem it harder for them to complete the mission at hand. The three of them headed into the hotel with two goons behind them. They took the elevator to the tenth floor and stopped when they got to room 1015.

"Y'all can stand outside the door, I'll take it from here," Remo told his goons.

The three of them walked into the room, and Remo instantly began to unzip his pants. The girls had him hot and horny from the club, and he wasn't about to waste any more time. He had been imagining them sucking and riding his dick since he seen them dancing. He knew he was in for one of the best freak-offs of his life.

"I gotta use the bathroom. All them drinks at the club got my bladder on full," Shayla stated, running off to the bathroom before anyone could say another word.

She turned on the sink and let it run while she sent out a text, letting the rest of her crew know the room number and the number of goons outside the door. She waited until she received a reply before flushing the toilet and washing her hands. By the time she had made it out the bathroom, Nikki was in front of Remo sexy dancing as he rubbed his shaft. Knowing this would be a great way to stall time, Shayla joined Nikki, putting on a show for Remo.

"One of y'all come over here and put this honey bone in yo mouth!" Remo called out.

Knowing neither one of them wanted Remo's dick nowhere near their lips, Shayla thought quick and came up with a response. "That sounds good as hell and I can't wait to taste it. But how 'bout you let us lead for a while? Just sit back, relax and watch us do things to each other before we do them to you."

Remo smiled and licked his lips eagerly. Although he'd had a few threesomes before, it was something about these two women that told him this would be one for the history books. Scooting back on the bed and resting his back on the headboard, he watched the two women undress each other. They moved slow and seductively, as Nikki stripped Shayla down to her panties and bra.

"Damn, y'all sexy as hell," Remo moaned, stroking his rock-hard manhood up and down. "Y'all need to take turns sitting on my face. My tongue needs to taste the both of you," he continued.

Shayla knew she couldn't do that. If Demo came in and saw her receiving oral sex from another man, he would go crazy. Shayla didn't want to die while on a mission trying to kill someone else. *Where the fuck are they? We ain't gonna be able to hold him off for long.* As soon as the thought went into her mind, Demo walked into the room.

"Surprise muthafucka," he announced, gun aimed directly for Remo's head.

"W-what the fuck?!" Remo yelled out, startled, as he scrambled to put his dick back in his pants. "Who the fuck are you?" Remo asked, confused. He knew he had goons outside his door and didn't know how this man was able to enter his room without him hearing anything.

"What you want? You want some money; I got that shit. You ain't have to come in with yo Mag up to get nothing from me. I take care of the streets. You could have just asked me. Or you want some bitches? I got two right here and many more where that came from. I can—"

"Nigga, shut the fuck up. I ain't here for no money or no bitches. I'm here cuz somebody put money on yo head. And I'm here to collect," Demo stated before pulling the trigger, sending Remo's brains all over the walls.

CHAPTER ELEVEN

Nakia had been running errands all day trying to get ready to bury her brother. She spared no expense to give Jalyn the most beautiful homegoing service anyone had ever seen. She was thankful she had her best friend by her side because she knew she could not have done this alone. With everything Nakia had going on, she thought she would break at any moment. However, she knew the moment she broke, so would her children, and she couldn't let that happen.

Once she left the funeral home, Nakia was ready to get back to her children. She just wanted to hug on them and feel the unconditional love they gave her. She wished Raphael was by her side during her moment of weakness; however, Nakia couldn't even trust him. She loved a man she didn't even know, brought a child into this world with him and, all the while, he was working with the people that were trying to kill her. How could her fairytale play out like this? Every time Nakia thought about it, tears fell.

Walking back into Simone's house and seeing Aden's smiling face gave Nakia the joy she needed. She took him out of the playpen and cuddled him close to her. The smell of the baby lotion that Simone put on him invaded Nakia's nostrils, as Aden cooed in her ear.

"Aww, you missed mommy, huh?" Nakia asked, kissing him softly on his cheek. "Let's go find your big brother and sister, so I can make some food," Nakia continued.

"Hey girl," Simone greeted Nakia as she walked into the living room. "I was just about to call you and see what you wanted from the Chinese Restaurant. Lexi requested that for dinner."

"I was just coming back to cook them something, you don't have to order anything."

"It's cool, Lexi gets what she wants over here. Plus, yo ass been out all day, you don't need to be cooking nothing. Relax, sis. I know these next few days are going to be very hard for you, so allow me to lighten the load as much as I can."

Nakia smiled; Simone always had her back, and, for that, Nakia would always have hers as well. "Then, Chinese it is. I'll take some shrimp lo mein with extra shrimp. I'm gonna go take a shower while we wait on the food." Nakia handed Aden to Simone and went into the bathroom.

She wished she could turn herself inside out and let the

water wash away the sorrows of her heart. Nakia knew she was to blame for the death of her brother, and she wished she could trade places with him. It was her that should have been shot dead in the street that day, and Nakia would have to live the rest of her days knowing that. A life without her brother was a life she didn't want to live. Nakia knew that if it wasn't for the three children she had, she wouldn't be living at all.

Once she was out the shower and dressed in a pair of comfortable sweats, Nakia went into the living room. Simone was setting the dining room table and the children were sitting on the couch watching cartoons.

"Hey mommy," Lexi greeted, as they both jumped up to hug her.

"Hey y'all, I missed y'all so much today. What y'all watchin'?"

"Amazing World of Gumball. We missed you too," Rashaud replied.

"Do you wanna watch it with us, mommy?" Lexi asked, pulling Nakia over to the couch before she could even answer the question.

The doorbell rang, and Simone went to go retrieve the food, walking back in with two huge brown paper bags.

"Dang girl, what did you order, the whole menu?" Nakia joked.

"Well, I wanted to make sure everyone got enough to eat. It's still early and you know after you eat Chinese food, you're hungry thirty minutes later."

"Yeah, I guess you're right about that. Come on y'all, let's eat. We can watch cartoons after."

They all sat around the table eating and laughing. This was the first time Nakia had laughed in days, as they all reminisced about Jalyn.

"Girl, I remember that time he called up to my job talking about Uncle Pookie died and I needed to get off early. Sis, he was crying and everything. He came and picked me up from work, and we went to a party in Ohio that night," Simone laughed.

"Girl, that dude was good at getting somebody out of work," Nakia stated, laughing just as hard as Simone.

"Who is Uncle Pookie? I don't think I ever met him before," Rashaud questioned.

"That's because there was no Uncle Pookie; your Uncle Jalyn was just silly like that. He could make up a story at the drop of a dime and everyone would think it was the truth," Simone answered.

After dinner, Nakia sent her children to take showers while she helped Simone wash the dishes, promising them they would binge-watch Gumball when they were done.

"Have you spoke to Raphael today?" Simone asked once she was sure the children were upstairs.

"Nah, and I'm not sure if I even want to talk to him. How can I trust him, sis? He blames me for his parents being murdered. His people were the reason I was in the hospital, and my son and I almost didn't come out of that. Aden was in the hospital for weeks, Simone. What if Raphael had killed Bailey that night? It's just so much that plays into this."

"Yeah, but you can't never not talk to him. Y'all have a son together. What are you gonna do when Rashaud and Lexi start asking questions? He's the only man they even seen you in a relationship with other than their father. And, besides, I know he would want to go to Jalyn's funeral. He loved him too," Simone spoke.

"I haven't even made it that far sis. I feel so broken without Jalyn. If he was here right now, he would have all the answers."

Tears fell from her eyes quicker than she could wipe them away. Simone rushed over and wrapped her arms around Nakia. She wasn't trying to be hard on her friend; she just wanted her to be ready for everything she would go through after this. Things were about to be hard for Nakia, and Simone wanted her to be able to take on everything that was about to come her way.

"I'm sorry girl, I didn't mean to…"

"No, don't be sorry. You ain't doing shit but telling the truth. It's okay," Nakia replied. "I will call him tomorrow and tell him about the funeral arrangements. You're right; I know both him and Rosa would want to be there. It's just hard for me. I don't blame Raphael for Jalyn being murdered. I know that was all me, I take all that. But, at the same time, it was his people that killed him. This shit is just so fucked up," she continued.

"Yeah, I feel you on that shit. I wish I could take all this away. I'm sorry friend."

Boom! Boom! Boom!

The hard banging at the door shook them out of their deep conversation. They looked at each other in confusion.

"Are you expecting someone?" Nakia whispered. When Simone shook her head no, Nakia whispered for her to look and see if she knew who the person was. She also told her not to open the door until she came back. The banging continued, as Nakia scooped Aden into her arms and ran upstairs.

"Mommy, who is that beatin' on the door like that?" Rashaud asked, walking out of the bathroom and meeting Nakia in the hallway.

"I don't know yet, but I need you to keep your sister and brother in the room and be very quiet. Don't come out until I come in and get y'all." Nakia handed Aden to Rashaud and followed him into the room with Lexi.

"Mommy, who's that?" Lexi asked.

"I'm about to find out. Sit down and don't make a sound. I'll be back in a minute."

Nakia ran into the room she was staying in and grabbed the gun Raphael had given her from the nightstand drawer. Taking it off safety, she ran back down to Simone.

"I don't know who that man is," Simone mouthed.

Nakia looked out the door at the tall man dressed in dark jeans and a red hoodie. He had his hood over his head, but his long dreads hung out from each side. Nakia had never seen the man in her life either, so she knew damn well they were not about to open the door for him.

"Go get your phone and call Raphael," Simone suggested.

Nakia nodded her head and ran to the living room. Simone watched, as the man walked back to his car, pulled something out and tucked it into his pants. Simone's eyes widened as she feared the man had a gun. He walked back to the door and began banging again while simultaneously calling someone on the phone.

"Raphael ain't answering; I've called him three times," Nakia whispered as she walked back to the door.

"Bitch, I think this nigga got a gun. He went back to his car and tucked something in his jeans," Simone informed.

Nakia's heart beat fast and hard as she worried about her next move. Was this the end? Did the man that killed her brother finally find her? All three of her children were upstairs, and she would be damned if she allowed anyone to harm them. She would protect them at any cost, even if that meant joining her brother in death.

"Do you have any weapons in here?" Nakia whispered.

Before Simone could answer, Nakia's phone began to vibrate. Looking at it and seeing it was Raphael, Nakia quickly answered.

"Raphael, it's a man outside beating on the door, and Simone says she thinks he has a gun. I got my gun, but I'm scared."

"Nakia, calm down and breathe. That's my homeboy, I

sent him to y'all. His name is Josh and he gonna take y'all to a hotel. Let him in; he just called me and told me y'all didn't open the door," Raphael replied

Simone saw the worried look ease from Nakia's face, as Nakia nodded to her to open the door.

"Why do we have to go to a hotel Raphael? What's wrong with us being here at Simone's house?" Nakia asked.

"Look, some shit popped off and I'm pretty sure Manny knows where y'all are. I can't take no chances of y'all getting hurt. Get the kids, and you and Simone get out of there. Once y'all at the room, call me, and I'll bring y'all everything y'all need. Just hurry up and get out of there."

"What? How does Manny know where we are?" Nakia asked, confused as she watched Josh step into the house.

"I'll explain all that when I come see you. Just get out the house now!" Raphael spoke before hanging up the phone.

"We gotta go now!" Nakia told Simone before running up the stairs to her children. Simone was right on her heels as they both ran up the stairs together.

"How does Manny know where I live?" Simone asked.

"I don't know. Raphael is gonna come to the hotel and talk to us. I don't know what's going on Simone, but we gotta go now."

Simone nodded, trusting what Nakia said, and went to grab her shoes and purse. Nakia burst through the door to see her children curled up on the floor. "Rashaud and Lexi, put your shoes and come on, we gotta go. Hurry up, I'll be back in two minutes."

Before they could say another word, Nakia rushed to her room, grabbing Aden's diaper bag and filling it with bottles and formula. She grabbed a pack of diapers before placing the gun inside the bag and zipping it up. She slipped on her Air Force Ones and went back to her children.

Simone was already in the room with the kids and was wrapping Aden in blankets. Josh was downstairs screaming for them to hurry. Nakia took Rashaud and Lexi by the hand and led them down stairs with Simone and Aden close by.

"Y'all ready? We gotta go now. We already wasted too much time and I don't know how much more we got. That nigga could be on his way right now," Josh informed.

"Mommy, who is this?" Lexi asked.

"This is Raphael's friend and he's gonna take us to a hotel. It's gonna be fun like a mini vacation."

Josh opened the door, and the group walked out and headed towards Josh's black Tahoe. Lexi and Rashaud climbed back to the third row and put on their seat belts while Josh placed the bags they did bring out into his trunk. Once everyone he'd come to get were safely in the car, Josh opened the driver's door. Everything happened so fast that Nakia barely had time to react. The shots scared them so bad that all the children began to cry. Simone screamed as she watched Josh's body fall limp.

Thinking quick on her feet, Nakia jumped to the driver's

seat and started the engine. Her fight or flight instinct kicked in and she knew she had to protect her children. There was no way they were dying right now, not like this. There were so many shots coming at the truck that Nakia couldn't tell where they were even coming from.

"Get on the floor!" Nakia yelled to her kids as she tried her best to get away from the bullets. She pulled out the driveway as fast as she could. The only windows that were left in the Tahoe was the windshield and the driver's side window. The rest had been shattered as the bullets hit them.

"Simone, call Raphael! Tell him what's going on and tell him a car is still following us," Nakia called out as she navigated the Tahoe through the streets.

"I can't, my phone is in my purse and Josh put that in the trunk."

"Fuck, mine is too! Nakia yelled.

"Mommy, I'm scared. Why are they shooting at us?" Lexi asked frantically.

Lexi shook in fear so badly as her mother drove so fast, she could barely keep her tiny body from sliding across the floor. Rashaud was in complete shock as silent tears fell from his eyes. Nakia knew her children were terrified just as she was, and her only goal was getting them to safety. She drove as fast as she could, but the car was still right on her tail. No matter where she turned, they were still right behind her.

Then, as if God had sent Nakia an angel, she spotted two police cars sitting at a Tim Horton's at the corner of the street.

Turning inside the parking lot, Nakia pulled right alongside the chatting officers. Screaming as soon as she rolled down the only remaining window of the SUV, the officers looked in her direction. Before she could say anything, the car slowed down right in front of the coffee shop and started firing bullets. Nakia yelled for everyone in the car to take cover as she saw one of the officers fall dead right before her eyes.

Nakia felt trapped and scared for the lives of her children. She heard one of the officers call in the shooting and heard the cars as they sped off in pursuit of the shooters. As soon as they did, Nakia lifted her head up and exited the parking lot, going the opposite way of the chase. Within minutes, she was pulling into the parking lot of a 24-hour CVS.

"Come on y'all," Nakia ordered.

"What we doing?" Simone asked, confused, as she looked around at the empty parking lot.

Nakia was already in the trunk grabbing her purse and her son's diaper bag. "I'm about to order an Uber; we have to get out of this car. It's shot the hell up and whoever was shooting at us knows the type of car we are in."

Simone nodded and exited the car. They all walked into the store and browsed the aisles as they waited on the car. It was the longest seven minutes of Nakia's life; however, when the Uber did arrive and they were all safely inside, Nakia was able to breathe. She was happy that they all made it out alive and unharmed.

They pulled into the parking lot of the Atheneum Hotel,

and Nakia rented the penthouse suite for the entire week. She didn't know how long they would have to be there, but she wanted to assure they all had enough room to be comfortable. Once they were in the room, Nakia called Raphael and told him what happened. Just as Nakia knew, he was livid and was at the hotel room within fifteen minutes.

"Oh, my God, are y'all alright?" Raphael asked as soon as he walked into the door.

"Yeah, we're good, just a little shaken up but, thankfully, none of us got hurt. I can't say the same for the dude you sent to come get us. He's dead in front of the house," Nakia informed.

"Man, what the fuck! Imma get someone over there to clean that up. Look, I don't know how many niggas Manny got on his payroll, but what I do know is he gonna be sending all of them for us. I need y'all to stay here and not leave. I'll bring y'all anything y'all need, but y'all can't leave. I need to make sure y'all stay safe. I don't know what I would do if anything happened to you or the kids," Raphael stated.

"Stay here for how long? I can't stay here; I've already planned Jalyn's funeral," Nakia informed.

"You're gonna have to push that back or something Nakia. We talking life or death."

"Push it back, fuck you mean? These muthafuckas already stopped his life, now you want me to let them stop his funeral too? This shit is getting ridiculous Raphael."

"Look, Nakia, I'm just trying to keep you and the kids

safe. Right now, that is my only objective. I've done the same and pushed my parents' funeral back until I'm able to get at Manny. You're not the only one that lost someone. And unless you want someone out here planning your funeral the way you planned Jalyn's, then you will push it back!" Raphael yelled a bit harsher than he intended.

Nakia couldn't do anything but look at him with tears forming in her eyes. She couldn't believe how coldhearted Raphael was being. No more was he the loving fiancé she once had. Nakia didn't even know the man that was standing in front of her.

"Right, you want me to push my brother's funeral back because yo family of murderers are coming after us. You can't get yo family in line so, now, you want to stop me from burying mine. You know what Raphael, fuck you! I thought you were my blessing, the man that came into my life and changed everything. Yeah, you changed everything but not for the good. Yo ass is a curse, not no fuckin' blessing! Just get the fuck outta here."

"I'm the curse? Nakia, look around you; the only reason this situation even exists is because of you. You wanna sit here and blame me because that's easier for you to cope with. But, the truth is this never would have happened if you had never opened your mouth. I'm 'bout to get outta here; I can't deal with this shit. I got a couple niggas outside the hotel, so y'all are safe. They will also bring y'all anything y'all need," Raphael stated before walking out the door.

CHAPTER TWELVE

"Detective, at what point did you form the taskforce that was on my client's case?" the defense asked.

"The task force was started six years ago and we strictly work with sex trafficking cases. It is my job to get criminals like him off the streets," Deja answered.

"I see, and how many detectives are in this taskforce?"

"It's four of us."

"All women, correct?"

"Yes, it is in fact an all-female taskforce. Is that important?" Deja asked, seemingly confused by Kyree's line of questioning.

"Well, yes, it is. Detective, are you familiar with the definition of entrapment?"

"Objection! Your Honor, this is speculation!" the prosecutor yelled.

"Sustained! Mr. Lewis, rephrase the question," the judge stated.

"No need, I have no further questions," Kyree informed before taking his seat. He looked over at the jury, saw the looks on their faces and knew he'd done exactly what he wanted to do. Raising suspicion of a witness' intentions was always a good thing in his eyes, as long as the witness was for the prosecution.

"Detective, you worked very close with the defendant, correct?" the prosecutor asked.

"Yes, that is correct. Myself and the other three ladies in the taskforce. One of them worked closely with the defendant's brother," Deja answered.

"Are you referring to Detective Arion Adams?"

"Yes, she was drugged, beaten and held against her will by the defendant. I was also a witness to that."

"Can you tell me more about that night? The night you found Detective Adams?"

Deja went on telling the prosecutor everything that happened, making sure to look Russell directly in the eyes while she did so. She wanted Russell and all men like him to be put away, and she was gonna do everything in her power to make sure that happened. Deja gave her entire testimony to the courtroom from start to finish.

"So, to the defendant's knowledge, you were a sex worker that worked for him?"

"Yes, that is correct," Deja informed.

"Thank you, I have no further questions."

The judge let Deja know she could step down before allowing the prosecutor to call yet another witness. Bailey's hands shook as sweat covered them. She slowly walked to the stand, wishing she could turn around with every step. If she'd just kept her pact with Nakia and not come to testify, she wouldn't be going through this. Bailey could feel Russell's eyes staring daggers into her, slicing her with every blink.

"Miss Malone, can you tell the court your place of employment?" the prosecutor asked.

"Yes, at the Courtyard Marriott," Bailey replied.

"Is that the DTW location?"

"Yes, that is correct."

"Can you tell me how you met the defendant?"

"He was a guest at the hotel. At first, everything was normal, that was until my coworker and myself noticed that he was with two very young girls," Bailey informed.

"I see, can you tell me more about the events that took place at your job?"

Bailey went on answering the questions that both the prosecutor and defense asked her. When she was finally done, she felt as though a weight had been lifted from her shoulders. She walked out the stand feeling like she'd just saved the world. All the fear had left as she told her story. In Bailey's eyes, her testimony would assure that Russell would never see light of day again. Bailey walked back to the briefing room with her head held high. She grabbed her belongings and headed out to the car that would take her home.

Once she was at home and out of her court clothes, she called Nakia. She knew why Nakia wasn't at court; however, she still wanted to let her know what happened. They phone rung several times before going to voicemail. Instead of leaving a message, Bailey hung up and shot a text to Nakia before heading into the kitchen and finding her something to eat.

TIANNA WALKED out of the courtroom after hearing the Judge say, "Court is adjourned and will resume tomorrow morning at nine."

Seeing Russell had reopened wounds Tianna thought had long been healed. Everything in her wanted to jump over the bench and beat the shit out of Russell until he was no longer breathing. She thought that going to court and watching Russell receive his fate would be enough for her. However, it wasn't. Prison was way too good for Russell in Tianna's eyes. He needed to be in hell burning for everything he'd done to the people around him.

When Tianna returned home, she went straight to her room and took a shower. Her emotions were all over the place.

Tianna wanted to cry and kill all at the same time. Every horrible thing that happened in her adult years had been tied to Russell. The murder she'd committed, the drugs she'd consumed, all the running for her life. It had all been because of Russell.

"I fuckin' hate him!" Tianna yelled as she plopped down on her bed. Taking the half smoked blunt from her ashtray, Tianna lit it and took a deep pull, attempting to blow out all her problems as she exhaled.

"Hey, girl, you good?" Tiny asked, walking into Tianna's room.

"Not really, but I'll be okay. You know how you think you over shit, just to find out that you're not. I'm strong though, so I'll be good."

"It's the trial of that Russell dude, huh? Maybe you shouldn't go to the trial anymore. You don't need shit else bringing you down."

"Nah, sis, I gotta see how this plays out," Tianna stated. She wanted to be there when the judge handed down Russell's verdict. Hell, she needed to be there. She wanted to look in Russell's eyes before they walked him out the courtroom in chains. She wanted him to know that everything that was happening to him was karma for the way he'd treated women, including her.

"Yeah, I get exactly what you sayin'. I would feel the same way if the nigga that forced me into the trade was on trial.

How 'bout you let me come with you? It might be better if you're not there alone," Tiny offered.

"That's sweet, but I told you, this is something I have to do alone. Sometimes, the only way out of something is through it."

Tiny nodded her head, not wanting to push the issue any further. All she could do was be there for Tianna in the way that she would allow her to be. So, she let it go, giving Tianna a hug before she walked out of her room. Tiny was pregnant, so her hormones made her want to do more than just sit around and watch the only person she had left hurt. She knew she had to do something about this, even if Tianna didn't know about it.

Tiny thought back as she remembered her ex always talking about some assassins nicknamed 'the crew'. She remembered him going on the black market to contact them whenever he needed someone taken care of. She was gonna find them and put a price on Russell's head. *Don't worry Tianna, I got you.*

THE CREW PULLED up to Feez's home and exited the SUV. It was late afternoon and they were all tired from being up all night after the mission. All anyone wanted to do was split the money and go to sleep.

"You did your thing on the mission Jania, for real," Shayla

complimented.

"Yeah, for this to be your first mission, it was executed flawlessly. You're clearly a natural and fit right in with the crew," Demo reiterated.

"Awww, thank y'all. But y'all are what made it so easy for me. I didn't think I was gonna be able to do the shit at first, but y'all made it fun; plus, I'm making money. Shit don't get no better than this," Nikki responded. "I can't wait for us to go on our next mission," she continued.

Feez looked over at her and smiled. Not only was she sexy but she was a hustler as well. Feez loved that shit. Feez had been feeling Nikki, or Jania as he called her, since the first time he'd laid eyes on her. So, once everyone else was ready to go, he asked Nikki to stay with him, assuring her that he would take her back to her hotel room. She agreed, saying her goodbyes to the crew before they walked out the door.

"Do you want anything to drink?" Feez asked.

"Yes, I'll take a bottled water," she responded.

Nikki was feeling Feez as well; however, she had way too much going on to rush into anything at the moment. Nikki had a lot of secrets she wasn't ready to reveal yet. She couldn't have anything fucking up her money, and she was scared that her secret would do just that. Although she wanted to tell Feez, she decided to hold it in until she could no longer do so. Nikki was still not showing but knew she would be in a few weeks. She knew she would need to do as many missions as she could to stack her money, just in case they told her she couldn't work with them while being pregnant.

"So, how do you really feel?" Fee asked, handing Nikki her bottle of water.

"What do you mean? Nikki asked, confused.

"I mean, about the mission, tell me how you really feel about that. I mean, I know you told the rest of the crew you was down with it, but is that how you really feel?" Feez took a seat on the couch across from Nikki and waited for her response.

"It was cool for real. It was like an adrenaline rush; plus, I'm makin' money. This shit works for me."

"Good, cuz I kinda like having you around," Feez responded.

Nikki smiled, being happy to be around as well. Her life had changed for the better since she'd met Feez, and he didn't even know it. She didn't have anyone besides the baby she was carrying, so to be able to call 'the crew' family was a luxury she was thrilled to have.

"You know, you don't have to stay in that hotel room anymore. I have plenty of space for you to stay here until you find a place of your own," Feez offered.

"That's sweet Feez, but I could never impose."

Feez stood up, walked over to the loveseat Nikki was sitting on, and sat next to her. Taking her hand into his, he spoke again, "You're not imposing on anything, I offered. And if you accept, I would love to have you here with me."

Feez gently placed his finger under her chin and turned her head, so she could look into his eyes. He wanted her to see that he was indeed being genuine. "I promise, I don't want anything in return; I just want to help. You're family now, and family don't stay in no damn hotel. You can have one of my guest rooms, and it's up to you how long you want to stay here. If you like being here, you can stay; if not, you can leave. It's no pressure, and everything is up to you."

Nikki looked into Feez's eyes and something about them told Nikki he was being honest. She didn't think he would play her or hurt her in any way. So, with that, she wanted to say yes; however, she knew if she did, then she would have to tell him about her pregnancy. There was no way she would be able to hide it from him while she lived with him.

"If I do move in with you, what does that mean?" Nikki asked.

"It would mean that you wouldn't be staying in a hotel. I'll be honest; I'm not comfortable with you going on missions, then going back to a hotel room alone. This is all new to you, so I would just be more comfortable with you here. That way, I know you're safe."

"That's sweet you wanna keep me safe. You must care about me."

"I do care," Feez admitted.

"I'll tell you what, I'll stay here tonight and see how it goes. Give me a little time to think things over. Then, tomorrow, I will give you my answer."

"That's cool with me. Come on, let me show you to your room," Feez said, motioning for Nikki to follow him.

She followed Feez up the stairs and down the hall until they reached the room Nikki would be staying in. He opened the door, and Nikki walked into the most beautiful bedroom she'd ever seen. It was decorated in all white everything, from the furniture to the pictures on the wall. Everything was as white as snow. The only color in the room were the many green plants that hung from the wall or sat in beautiful white vases in the corners. The room was giving princess treatment, and Nikki loved it.

Nikki got settled into her new room, taking a long hot shower. Once she was finished, she slipped into one of the many white t-shirts that was folded neatly inside the dresser. She was just about to get into the bed when Feez knocked on the door. She opened the door and smiled at the plate of food he was holding. Nikki opened the door wider and allowed Feez access.

"I didn't know if you were hungry or not, but I was. So, I made a couple of BLT's. It's not a gourmet meal or anything, but I do make a dog ass BLT," Feez laughed.

"That's funny because BLT's are my favorite," Nikki stated, taking the plate from Feez.

"Well, Imma let you eat and get some sleep. I'll see you when I wake up."

Once she was done eating, Nikki crawled into bed, curling up under the covers and slipping into a deep sleep. It was the first deep sleep she'd gotten in months. She hadn't slept this well since before Cole started beating on her. It felt good to finally have a sense of safety. It had been so long since she'd felt safe anywhere, especially around a man. However, for some reason, Nikki felt safe with Feez. Even though he didn't know her real name, she knew he would never let anything happen to her. That was a feeling that Nikki didn't want to let go. So, when she finally woke up the next morning, Nikki decided to tell Feez that she would stay with him.

CHAPTER THIRTEEN

Nakia stood in the mirror looking at her reflection. All she could wonder was why? Why had she not listened to Jaylen when he said not to call the police? Why did she go to the club with Simone the night she'd met Raphael? More importantly, why did she fall in love with him? How could she not know who he was? He'd been the enemy this entire time and, all the while, Nakia had been sleeping with him. He and his entire family were impostors, and Nakia had a child with him. A beautiful baby boy whom Nakia loved dearly. A baby whom Nakia once thought was made with love. However, she now knew that he was made in the mist of tragedy.

Nakia sighed, wishing she could just wake up from this horrible dream. *How can I ever trust Raphael with my son? If I keep my son away from him, how will I explain that to Aden?*

Nakia thought, trying to figure out a way for her not to be the bad guy. She had so much going on at once that she couldn't even focus on one thing at a time. Tears fell from her eyes, and she wanted to scream out loud to let out all of her frustrations. However, her children were in the next room, and she knew they would hear her. Nakia couldn't let her children see or hear her break down. In order to seem strong for her children, Nakia kept her emotions bottled up inside.

Nakia heard a soft knock at the door and quickly wiped her tears in an effort to pull herself together. She opened the door smiling as if she wasn't just crying a few seconds before.

"Hey girl, you good?" Simone asked, walking into Nakia's room. She sat on the bed and put her feet up, making herself more comfortable.

"I'm fucked up, sis. Everything is so fucked up. Raphael is on bullshit, wanting me to push Jalyn's funeral back til I don't even know when. I'm just so fuckin' over this shit. I don't even know what to think. I used to love this man, so much so that I gave him a fuckin' son. Only to find out his fuckin' family is trying to kill me," Nakia whispered, not wanting the children to overhear.

Simone stood to her feet and opened her arms, bringing Nakia in for a hug. She wished she could rewind time and take away all the pain her best friend was feeling, but that wasn't reality. The reality was that all of this had really happened, and there was no turning back. Simone hated that for Nakia but vowed to be there for her through it all.

"Why does he want you to reschedule the funeral?" Simone asked, confused.

"He thinks that if I have the funeral now, then I would be a target. He thinks his cousin would be there to kill me."

"Well, friend, you know I'm on yo side and everything, right? However, I don't disagree with Raphael on that one. Just hear me out sis; that nigga was just trying to kill us at my house. How did he even know you were there? That nigga can clearly find you anywhere and send someone for you. Bitch, this shit is scary. So, maybe it's not such a bad idea to postpone the funeral. Only for a little while and maybe change the location."

"How the hell can I do that? I'm the reason Jay is dead in the first place Simone. I caused all this shit." Nakia managed to say, bawling uncontrollably as she spoke. "He told me not to do it, not to get involved, and my stupid ass did it anyway. Now, look, my fuckin' brother is gone. And I gotta continue on with life knowing it was all my fault," Nakia cried, looking Simone directly in her eyes.

"No, friend, that's what you not gonna do. I'm not about to sit around and let you continue to blame yourself for any of this. You did the right thing and called the police. You only did what any normal person would do. You saved those little girls, Nakia. They were young, and that grown ass man was taking advantage of them. If you didn't call the police, they would still be in that life or, even worse, dead."

"I know, but..."

"There is no but Nakia, you're a hero more than anything. If it was Lexi out here like that, you would want someone to do exactly what you did and call the police, correct?" Simone asked, attempting to prove to Nakia that she'd done the right thing.

Nakia didn't want to hear that she'd saved strangers. She'd put the lives of people she didn't even know over her own brother's. While she may have been a hero to them, she felt like the enemy to her own blood.

"You're right, I did save those young girls. However, I wished I could have saved my brother. I would have rathered it that way than anything else. All I keep hearing in my head is him saying *stay out of it, Kia*, and I couldn't even do that. Now, he's gone. His funeral is supposed to be tomorrow and I can't even make that happen. I'm failin' him, Simone."

Nakia cried as she thought back on the days leading up to Jalyn's death. The last few moments she had left with her brother were spent chasing after Raphael, trying to beg him to stay. If she would have just let his ass go, Jalyn would still be alive. It was Raphael's family that killed Jalyn in the first place. So, in Nakia's eyes, Raphael was just as guilty as she was.

"You didn't fail him at all, Nakia. Jalyn knew just how much you loved him. Believe me, I was on the outside looking in on that shit, and even I felt it. I can see him in heaven now cussin' you out because you down here blaming yourself. Stop that shit, Nakia. You're gonna bring yourself into a depression that you're not gonna be able to get out of."

Simone didn't mean to sound harsh at all; she just loved her best friend and hated seeing her in so much pain. Simone couldn't imagine going through the type of pain Nakia was going through; however, Nakia had children to live for, and Simone wanted to make sure she did so.

"Now, as far as Raphael goes, I don't know what to tell you about that. His ass his clearly crazy. You on yo own with that one, sis. You already know Imma tell you to leave his ass." Simone busted out into laughter. She laughed so hard that Nakia couldn't help but join her.

"Yeah, him and his family are crazy. It's giving very much Boyz In The Hood, the way they all around here toting guns and shooting everybody up."

"Right, the Albanian version bitch," Simone joked.

Nakia laughed so hard, she almost fell over. She hadn't laughed like that in weeks, and she was glad that Simone was by her side through all this. Without her, Nakia didn't know where she would be without her best friend.

"Come on bitch, let's raid that minibar. Everything that's going on gives us an excuse to day drink," Simone suggested.

Nakia didn't say a word as she followed Simone to the bar where they both poured up their sorrows. The children were all preoccupied with cartoons. While she wasn't gonna have too many drinks, she was definitely going to get tipsy.

Manny walked out of O'shay's parents' home, wishing it

was a trip he didn't have to make. Out of all the goons that could have been at the spot that day, Manny was sick that it was O'shay. He didn't deserve what he got, and Manny was gonna bring a little extra pain when he killed Raphael because of it. He knew nothing he did would bring O'shay back. However, he hoped the hundred thousand dollars he'd just dropped off to his parents would help lighten the load. Manny had just gotten back in his car when his phone rung.

"What up doe?" Manny answered.

"Yooo, Manny, I got eyes on Raphael's sister; what you want me to do?" Javon spoke.

"Where y'all at?"

"She just walked into Sommerset," he replied.

"Cool, I'm on my way. Stay on her and text me if anything changes."

Manny started his car and pulled off swiftly. If he couldn't get to Raphael, then he for damn sure was gonna bring Raphael to him. He was wreaking havoc on all of them exactly the way he told Niko he would. He knew his brother was looking down on him, smiling at the way he was avenging his death. Manny promised he wouldn't rest until everyone had gotten what they deserved.

His trigger finger itched as he did ninety miles an hour, trying to make it to Sommerset mall before Rosa left. He had plans for that bitch, and she didn't even know it. Rosa was gonna lead Manny to Raphael one way or another. Either by choice or force and it was up to her to decide which one.

Twenty minutes later, Manny was pulling into the parking lot, calling Javon as soon as he parked. Javon let Manny know that he was still on her head, and she was now in Victoria's Secret purchasing underwear.

"Cool, I'm outside, we bout to get this bitch."

"She not alone though; she got some big nigga with her. I could take him out right now bro, but that might cause some problems for us," Javon stated.

"Nah dawg, don't do that. I don't even want them seeing us coming until it's too late," Manny responded.

"Okay cool, I got you. She just left out the store. Imma keep following her and let you know when she gets ready to leave the mall."

"Fasho, just make sure that you don't get spotted. I don't want them muthafuckas to know shit until it's too late," Manny reiterated.

Rosa loved to shop. It was one of her favorite things to do in her spare time. However, today wasn't retail therapy at all, seeing how she was shopping for the unthinkable. Rosa was preparing for the funerals of the man she loved and both her parents all at the same time. Rosa wouldn't wish the pain she was feeling on anyone, not even her worst enemy. This was too much for one person to bear, and Rosa didn't even know how she was still walking around with a straight head.

Rosa hated the fact that Raphael had postponed their parents' funeral because of Manny. He'd been the one to kill them and, now, Raphael and Rosa couldn't put their parents to rest because of him. Rosa knew Manny was a huge problem that needed to be solved quickly. *I gotta kill that nigga myself and with my bare hands if I have to,* Rosa thought. She wanted nothing more than to kill Manny and anyone that was working with him slowly. Rosa wanted to make Manny suffer the same way she was suffering. After buying everything she needed for the two funeral services that she would have to attend, she told Stretch she was ready to leave.

Stretch was Rosa's personal bodyguard who'd been working for her family for over ten years. Rosa always felt safe with Stretch because she knew he would never let anything happen to her. Standing six feet seven inches tall and three hundred pounds of pure muscle, his own two hands were registered as lethal weapons. So, if his huge frame didn't scare a nigga off, then his trigger finger damn sure would. He was a beast with the pistol and with his marksman aim; he could hit any target within two hundred yards. Anyone who fucked with Stretch was crazy to do so, and everyone knew it.

"You wanna get something to eat Stretch?" Rosa asked. She hadn't had an appetite in days and was surprised at herself for even being hungry.

"You know me, I can always eat," Stretch answered with a laugh.

"What you got in mind?" he continued.

"I think I'm feeling pasta, nothing fancy thought. Let's just go to an Olive Garden or something."

"Olive Garden is the shit while you playing. I ain't believe you even want something like that. I just knew your ass was gonna say steak and lobster," Stretch joked.

"Nigga, you trying to call me bougie?" Rosa laughed.

"I mean, I wasn't gonna say it straight out like that but since you did—"

"Hahahaha, very funny. I ain't bougie at all. I love Olive Garden; it's actually bussin', and that's why I wanted to go there."

Stretch laughed as he walked alongside Rosa. He was unaware of the danger they were both in. Making his way to the exit door, he had Rosa stop, so he could Google the nearest Olive Garden restaurant, not wanting to sit still in the car to GPS it.

"Stretch, I think someone is following us," Rosa whispered, not wanting anyone else to overhear her.

"You talking 'bout dude in the white shirt? I peeped him a few stores back, but I wasn't sure if he was really following us. But I noticed a few minutes before you said something that he was."

Rosa placed her hand in her purse and took her gun off safety. She wanted to be prepared for whatever was about to go down. She eyed the man, as he sat at a bench across from where they stood.

"What you wanna do?" Rosa asked, being down for whatever.

"Shit, we gonna walk out that door. I hope that nigga don't want no smoke cuz if he does, I got that Za for his ass."

"Do you think he's a part of Manny's crew?" Rosa asked.

"I'm not sure but, if that nigga tries anything, his ass is dead. You know I'm not gonna let anything happen to you."

"Oh, I'm already hip. I got my gun too, so you already know I got yo back."

Rosa and Stretch walked out the door with Javon right behind them. Rosa already knew what was up. Manny had found her and put a play down to kill her. She wasn't gonna act like she wasn't scared because she was. Manny had taken out everyone she loved with ease, so she knew he stood on business. However, one thing for sure and two things for certain, Rosa wasn't going down without a fight. If Manny wanted to get at her, he was gonna have to put in some work, and Rosa would stand on that.

Javon texted Manny, letting him know that they were leaving the mall. Manny let Javon know he already had eyes on them and was ready. Javon looked around, making sure no one else was around. He didn't want to have any witnesses that he would have to come back for later. He was just about to pull his gun when he felt something around his neck, cutting off his air supply. He tried to scream for Manny, but there was no air left in his lungs.

He grabbed and scratched at the man's arm in an effort to free himself. However, it was to no avail. The grip the man had around his neck was much too strong. Manny, seeing his homeboy in distress, upped his Mag and fired two shots in their direction. Stretch instinctively placed Rosa behind his back while simultaneously pulling out his pistol. Looking back at the man they knew was following them, Stretch saw his younger brother Cash with the man in a chokehold.

"Bro, somebody shootin'!" Cash yelled.

Rosa, who already had her hand on her gun, upped it, not knowing what direction to point it in. She didn't know where Cash even came from, but she was happy he was there, especially with more than one person coming after them. Rosa wasn't sure how many shooters Manny had on them, so they needed as many hands on deck as they could.

Manny fired his gun again once he noticed Cash still had Javon in his grasp, shooting Cash in his leg. Cash screamed out in pain, letting Javon go and sending him falling to the concrete. Both Stretch and Rosa began firing in the direction the gunshots came from. Although they didn't see a shooter, they shot out several car windows in the process.

"We gotta get out of here; I know the police gotta be on their way by now. We in Troy, so you know someone called it in as soon as they heard the first shot!" Stretch yelled out.

Cash was already making his way towards them, trying his best to do so with one leg. Rosa covered them, firing shot after shot as stretch put Cash into the back seat. Manny couldn't even stand up to fire back with the ruthless way Rosa was shooting. He heard the shots stop and was just standing to fire back at them when he saw Rosa's car peel out the parking lot.

"Bro, hurry up and get in the car, they gettin' away!" Manny yelled.

Javon made his way over to the car as quickly as he could, still quite dazed from being put to sleep. He was pissed from being caught off guard the way he was, and he was also embarrassed. Here he was thinking he had one up on them when, in reality, they had plotted on him. Once Javon was in the car, Manny pulled off in search of Rosa and her minions.

"Lil bro, where the hell did you even come from?" Stretch asked, making his way down Big Beaver Road.

"I was already there doing some shopping when I saw y'all there. I was gonna come speak and, then, I saw ol' boy following y'all. So, I decided to stay back and peep the scene," Cash replied through his pain.

"Stretch, we need to get him to a hospital. He's losing a lot of blood!" Rosa yelled.

"No! I ain't doing no hospitals! Hospitals brings questions and police, and I'm not dealing with either today!" Cash yelled before Stretch could even reply. "Just take me to Tank; he will get me together," Cash continued.

"Cash, you're losing too much blood. I don't even think we can make it to Tank's place," Rosa tried to reason.

Tank was a friend of the family that had been around for years. He was a doctor in the war, which was how he got the name Tank because he drove in a huge tank everywhere he went. Cash had been hit in the thigh and, no matter how much pressure Rosa applied to the wound, it was still pouring blood.

"Stretch, we need to get him to a hospital before he bleeds out!" Rosa yelled.

"No, Stretch! No fuckin' hospitals, Tank only!" Cash yelled, and Stretch knew he meant it.

Stretch was confused, torn between what his brother said he wanted versus what Rosa said he needed. He looked at Cash in the rearview mirror and saw the amount of blood he was losing. It was then that he decided he would take Cash to the nearest hospital. He couldn't have his brother dying right in front of him, and that's exactly what would happen if he drove all the way to Tank's house.

Stretch had just turned the corner when he noticed a car following them. Thinking quickly, he turned another corner and merged onto the freeway, looking into his mirror at the same car merging with him. He knew then it was Manny following them.

"Where the hell are you going? He's losing too much blood! He's gonna die if you drive all the way to Tank's house, take him to the fuckin' hospital!" Rosa yelled. She didn't want Cash to die, and she couldn't understand why Stretch wasn't listening to her.

"I hear you, and we're going to the hospital, but I can't stop right now. If I stop right now, then we all dead. This freeway is the only thing keeping us alive."

"What the fuck are you talking about?" Rosa asked, confused.

She tied Cash's t-shirt around his thigh as tight as she could, and the white shirt quickly became stained with crimson. Her heart beat fast and her hands shook, scared that she could not stop the bleeding.

"We got company. Manny is right behind us and I'm out of bullets. What you got in the clip?" Stretch asked. He didn't know how much fire power Manny had behind him, so he wasn't taking any chances. His goal was to get them all out of harm's way and get his brother to the hospital safely.

Rosa looked out the back windshield and, sure enough, Manny was on their tail. He was so closed behind them that if they made any sudden stops, he would for sure crash into the back of them. This entire time, Rosa couldn't wait to catch up with Manny. She'd talked so tough up until today and, now, she was scared. She never thought that Manny would be the one to come after her first. Rosa had a vision of how things were supposed to play out, and this was not it at all.

In Rosa's mind, she would hunt him down with Raphael by her side and a team of goons behind them. When they found him, they would torture him for hours before finally killing him. However, by the looks of things, that was not how things were going to play out.

"I got five bullets left; she can still make some shit shake with that," Rosa replied.

"Call Raphael and tell him what's going on; we don't know what this nigga coming with."

Stretch swerved between lanes in an effort to lose Manny but, no matter what he did, Manny was still behind them.

Picking up speed, Stretch veered over to the far-left lane and got off the freeway.

"Fuck!" Stretch yelled when Manny got off the freeway right along with them.

Rosa turned around and saw Manny right behind them. She bit her bottom lip as she tried to find Raphael's number with shaky hands. Rosa screamed when Manny hit her car with his, causing her to jerk forward and drop her phone. Cash attempted to grab his gun but to no avail; the blood he was losing had caused him to become extremely weak.

Get yourself together bitch, it's time to stand on business. Rosa tried to geek herself up. Reaching down to grab her phone, she quickly placed a call to Raphael. Manny hit their car once more just as Raphael answered.

"Bro, I'm in the car with Stretch and Cash, and Manny on us real bad. Cash is shot and it's not lookin' good at all!" Rosa yelled, pacing her phone on speaker.

"Fuck, where the fuck y'all at?" Raphael asked.

Stretch answered while Rosa rolled down the back passenger window. She pointed her gun at Manny's car and began firing shots. However, Stretch was driving so fast and wild that she couldn't get a clean shot.

"Keep him on y'all trail; I'm on my way right now," Raphael replied.

"We can't keep driving; Cash is losing too much blood. If we don't get him to a hospital soon, he's gonna die," Rosa stated.

Just as the words left Rosa's mouth, Manny hit their car with so much force that their car flipped twice, causing the car to collide with an abandoned building before it stopped flipping, leaving everyone inside unconscious.

Manny jumped out of his car gun in hand. He walked over to the car slowly, not knowing if he was walking into an ambush. However, once he got close enough to notice there was no threat, he was able to breathe. Cash was in the back seat with Rosa and he was clearly dead. Manny had saw enough dead bodies in his lifetime to know what one looked like, so he didn't need a doctor to call it. Stretch and Rosa were still alive however, both laid out from the impact. Manny called Javon over, and they both pulled Rosa out the car.

"Open the truck," Manny ordered before placing Rosa inside.

"Go take care of the nigga in the driver's seat," Manny continued.

He knew the police had to be on their way. He knew if nobody reported the crash, someone for damn sure reported the gunshots. They needed to be far away from the scene before any police or witnesses arrived. Without reservation, Javon walked over to the driver's side window and fired two shots into Stretch's head. Javon walked back over to the car and was just about to get in when a car pulled up behind them.

"Oh, my God, are y'all okay? This accident looks horrible," an older white man asked through his open window.

"Yeah, we good," Javon replied, waving to the man for him to continue on with his own business.

"You can be on your way now; we don't need anything," Manny stated.

"Are you sure? This looks pretty bad, and I don't mind helping. Does anyone in the other car need help? Does anyone need medical attention? I can at least call the police for y'all," the elderly man asked while opening his door and stepping out the car, not knowing the danger that awaited him.

"Yooo, just mind yo fuckin' business ol' man. We told you we good. Now, get back in yo fuckin' car and go wherever you was on yo way to!" Javon yelled, not wanting the old man to be hurt. However, he knew that's exactly what would have happened if he didn't leave at that moment.

Manny knew the longer they stayed at the scene, the harder it would be to get away. Manny wished the man would have just minded his own business, but they were past that point. Due to him being at the wrong place at the wrong time, the elderly man would suffer the same fate as Cash and Stretch. Manny upped his Mag and fired a single shot, the bullet piercing the man right between his eyes and sending him falling to the ground before he even knew what was happening.

CHAPTER FOURTEEN

Raphael placed several calls to Rosa, but they all went to her voicemail. He was in the area where Rosa said they were when he was on the phone with her. While it had only taken Raphael fifteen minutes to get there, he knew a lot could take place in fifteen minutes. Hanging up from his fifth failed attempt at calling, he called Stretch's phone. Raphael's heart dropped in his chest when Stretch's phone went to voicemail as well. He knew then that something was wrong.

"Fuck Rosa, not you too. I can't lose you too!" Raphael yelled, hitting his steering wheel in frustration. "I gotta find you, sis."

Raphael drove up and down block after block until his worst fears were confirmed. In the mist of about six police cars, a fire truck, and an ambulance was Rosa's Tesla, and it was totaled. Raphael could tell they had been in a horrible accident because it almost looked like it had been crushed. He also saw a body lying on the ground covered by a white sheet next to another car. Raphael could tell the car wasn't involved in the accident because it wasn't a scratch on it. *Who's car is this?* Once he got a bit closer to the scene, he knew the person lying on the ground had not been in a car accident but had been shot. There was a small circle on the person's head where the white sheet had become stained with blood. His palms became sweaty as he prayed to God that it wasn't Rosa underneath the sheet. Running towards the scene, Raphael was stopped in his tracks by one of the officers.

"Sir, this is a crime scene and is off limits to the public. You cannot cross the yellow type," the officer informed.

"This is my sister's car, where is she? Is this her laying on this cold ass ground like that?" Raphael screamed as he pointed over at the body.

"Your sister's car? What is your sister's name and are you sure this is her car?" the officer asked.

"Yes, I'm sure. She just called me about twenty minutes ago and let me know she was in this area."

Raphael gave the officer Rosa's information and description before he walked over to another plain clothes officer on the scene. They spoke for a moment before they both walked back over to Raphael. They asked Raphael a series of questions, all of which he pretended not to know the answer to before letting Russell know that Rosa had not been on the scene. However, three dead bodies were. The officer also explained to Raphael that if he had reason to believe his sister was in the car with the other victims, then he should go down to the station and file a missing person's report.

Raphael agreed before taking the card from the detective, getting into his vehicle and pulling off. He was desperate to find Rosa and knew that this day marked the beginning of the end for either him or Manny. The world was no longer big enough for the both of them to walk around in, not with them being on two different sides of the game. They were at war, and Raphael knew whoever lost would die, and he was okay with that. Grabbing his phone, Raphael frantically called Blue.

"What up doe, OG?" Blue answered cheerfully.

"That nigga Manny got Rosa," Raphael spoke.

"How long before you get here?"

"Bout twenty minutes."

"Cool, I'll be ready," Blue informed before disconnecting the call.

Raphael pulled up to Blue's spot exactly twenty minutes later. Blue was already standing in the door waiting on Raphael to arrive. Blue handed Raphael a duffle bag filled with guns as soon as he walked into the door.

"We gonna get her back, OG. Don't even stress. I know it's easier said than done, but we got this shit. That nigga ain't gonna be shit up against the fire power we got," Blue stated, trying to remain positive. Rosa was a good person and didn't deserve any of this. She didn't have anything to do with her family's dealings, and Blue hated she was caught in the middle of it. Blue knew that he would do anything to bring her home safely.

"Do you have any idea where to start lookin'?" Blue asked.

"We already went to his house and a couple of his spots. I know one more trap house he got over there in southwest. We can hit that one. I doubt he'll be there, but maybe one of the niggas over there will have some information about his whereabouts," Raphael replied.

Blue nodded his head in agreement with Raphael before walking out the door, duffle bags in hand. The mission they were on was personal for the both of them. Manny had killed both of Raphael's parents and now, probably, his sister. She was the only family he had left besides his son. However, since there was no trace of Rosa at the crime scene, they were unsure whether she was alive or not. Blue, who always looked at Rosa like a big sister, wanted to keep the faith that they would find Rosa and bring her back home alive. Either way, they both knew they were going to kill Manny for what he'd done.

Russell sat in his cell thinking about how he was gonna get out of the bullshit he'd gotten himself into. He knew that Fatbar had not killed all the witnesses due to the fact that one had come and stood trial. He'd placed so many calls to Fatbar, it was ridiculous, yet and still he'd not spoken with him. Russell couldn't help but to feel slighted by Fatbar's actions.

He contemplated having Kyree go find him and see what's going on but quickly decided against it. Russell knew exactly what was going on; Fatbar had played him.

"That muthafucka stole my money, I'm not sending anyone for him. I'm gonna handle this one myself," Russell said aloud.

An officer came to his door, and it buzzed before opening. The officer let Russell know his lawyer was there to visit him before cuffing him and walking him out of the cell. Russell was confused as to why Kyree was there to see him, seeing how trial wasn't set to resume until Monday. However, he kept a straight face as he walked down the hall towards the visitor's room.

Walking into the room, he sat down across from Kyree. Russell smiled, hoping Kyree had good news; however, the look on his face quickly told him otherwise. Kyree began to speak as soon as the officer left the room.

"We got a problem."

"What's wrong Kyree?"

"The prosecution has a high-profile witness that they're bringing in to testify on Monday. I have no idea who this witness is or what they could say against you."

"What do you mean by high-profile?" Russell questioned. He was confused about what Kyree was saying to him. How could they have a witness that he didn't know about and he was the lawyer? Something wasn't right, and they both knew it.

"That's what it said on the paperwork that was waiting for me when I got back to my office. There is no name on it, all it says is high-profile witness in bold letters," Kyree replied. "I need you to think about who this witness could be, so I can get some type of background on this person. I don't like coming into anything blindsided," he continued.

"What would deem a witness high-profile?" Russell asked, still confused.

Russell had no idea who this witness could be. He thought he knew everyone who could speak out against him; however, he was clearly wrong. While none of those people had been deemed high-profile, this one was.

"It would be a number of reasons. My guess is this is someone the police had in witness protection. Someone who they didn't want to be hurt if anyone found out they were going to testify. Do you have any idea who that could be?"

Russell thought for a half of a second before thinking of Fatbar almost instantly. *Maybe that's the reason I can't get in touch with him. This muthafucka done took my money and turned state's witness on my ass*, Russell thought before telling Kyree the exact same thing.

"And you think it's Fatbar just because he's not answering all of your calls? You do know that you're on trial for a number of charges?" Kyree asked.

Russell told Kyree everything, making sure not to leave anything out. If Fatbar wanted to take Russell down, he for damn sure wasn't going down alone. Fatbar had been in the business much longer than Russell. In fact, Fatbar was the one to teach Russell everything he knew. For him to flip on Russell was crazy; however, Russell knew in the business they were in, no one could be trusted.

"I'm going to look into this, but I highly doubt Fatbar is the high-profile witness the prosecution has. If you think of anyone else the high-profile witness could be, give me a call and I'll come see you. Never say anything about this over the phone," Kyree spoke before calling the guard and exiting the room.

Russell went back to his cell with a lot more to think about than he already had. Had Fatbar really become a witness against him? Russell couldn't see any other reason why Fatbar wouldn't answer his calls. Russell knew for a fact Fatbar had not had the witnesses taken care of, and that could be because he was a witness himself.

"How the fuck did I miss this shit? I thought Fatbar could be trusted because he had been like a father to me. He knew everything about me. If he testifies, then I'm for sure going down," Russell spoke.

Nikki woke up Saturday morning feeling refreshed. Feez had sent for all her things to be removed from the hotel room she was staying in and had them brought to his home. Once Nikki was showered and dressed for the day, she headed down to the kitchen for breakfast. She was going to prepare a breakfast for herself and Feez; however, when she got downstairs, she realized she was too late. Feez was already in the kitchen frying turkey bacon and scrambling eggs.

"Dang Feez, I was just about to come down here and cook breakfast for you," Nikki informed. "You've done so much for me already and I wanted to do a little something for you to show my appreciation," she continued.

"It's all good, you can cook breakfast tomorrow," Fee replied.

Once the food was done, the two of them sat at the table together and ate. Nikki was all smiles as she sat across from Feez as the lady of the house. Although they had only known each other for a short time and Feez had never said it, Nikki could feel that Feez loved her. It was a feeling that she'd never felt before, and it made her feel warm inside. However, there was still things she had yet to reveal to him.

The landline rang, and they both knew exactly what that meant. Feez stood up and walked over to the phone. He answered it and only said a few words during the minute-long conversation. Name, location, and a hundred and fifty thousand were the words he spoke. Nikki knew exactly what that meant as she smiled at the amount of money being charged. Once Feez hung up, he informed Nikki of the next mission, which was tomorrow in New York.

"Why don't you go call Shayla, and I'll call the rest of the crew about the mission?" Feez suggested.

Nikki nodded her head and went up to her room to get her phone. She found Shayla's number in her contacts and hit call.

"What up doe, Jania?" Shayla greeted.

"Hey girl, I'm calling to tell you about the mission tomorrow in New York."

"Bitch, why are you the one calling me and not Feez?" Shayla asked, confused.

"Feez asked me to call you while he called everyone else," Nikki responded.

"Yeah, okay. Let me find out you and Feez over there mixing business with pleasure," Shayla joked.

"Bitch, shut up. I am not about to play with you," Nikki laughed.

"I'll see yo ass tomorrow morning and, then, you gonna tell me everything," Shayla demanded before ending the call.

Nikki couldn't do anything but laugh at how nosy Shayla was. Feez came to Nikki's door a few moments later asking her to help him choose the Airbnb they would stay in. Nikki loved the way Feez included her in the decision-making of the mission. It made her feel special, and Nikki loved that.

The next morning, the entire crew met at Feez's house. They all sat in the living room, as Feez briefed them on the mission.

"It's a dude named Two and he a big money nigga in New York, a big-time plug. However, he fucked with the wrong nigga's family and now Two is a dead man. We leave in two hours, so, grab everything y'all gonna need to complete this mission," Feez said.

Once Feez was done, Shayla grabbed Nikki's hand and led

her to the kitchen so they could speak in private. Nikki giggled as they walked because she already knew what this was about.

"Okay, bitch, spill all the tea," Shayla said, taking a seat at the table.

"Girl, what are you talking about? It ain't shit to tell. Feez is just a nice guy. But that's something you already know, seeing how you've known him longer than I have."

"Cap! You can miss me with that he's just a nice guy bull-shit. Yeah, he's a nice guy, but I'm getting more than he's just a nice guy vibes. It's givin' y'all in love. I saw the way y'all was lookin' at each other in there, all googly eyed and shit. Y'all ain't fooling nobody but y'all selves with that shit," Shayla informed, not believing the explanation she was given.

Nikki busted out laughing. "Girl, yo ass is too much," Nikki joked.

"Maybe, but I'm right though. I love this for y'all, love is a beautiful thing. Just don't break his heart because then, Imma have to break you," Shayla said jokingly; however, Nikki knew she was serious.

The crew touched down in New York several hours later and went directly to their Airbnb. Just like before, they all found their rooms and met in the living room to discuss the layout of the plan. Once everything was in order, the crew changed into their all-black mission gear and headed out.

The mission seemed like it was an easy one to Nikki. They were on their way to Two's home where they were gonna kill him. It wouldn't take much for them to get inside the house.

Shayla was an extreme hacker and could get past any security system on the planet. The rest of them were shooters that could get past any security team on the planet.

The all black Nikki dressed in gave her a slimmer look, which she was thankful for, seeing how she was trying to hide her pregnancy. Although Nikki had yet to see a doctor, she'd done her own counting and knew that she was a little over three months along. Even though she wasn't showing yet, she knew it was just a matter of time before she would be. She knew she had to tell Feez; she just needed to save a little more money first.

After strapping herself up, she went down to join the rest of the crew in the living room before they all made their way out the door. Taking the drive to Brooklyn, they arrived at Two's house about thirty minutes later.

"Y'all ready?" Feez asked the crew.

"You know we stay ready," Regal responded, answering for them all.

Feez nodded his head, and they all exited the SUV. They cautiously walked the few blocks to Two's home. The house was rather big and sat on about a half-acre of land. There were no lights on in the yard, and they only had the front porch light to guide their way. They made their way to the back of the house, and Shayla walked up to the back door. Placing a small device up to the key pad, she punched in a few buttons. A few moments later, a green light shined on the keypad, letting them know that the code had been entered correctly.

"Damn bitch, you a beast with that shit," Nikki whispered.

"This what I do," Shayla smirked.

With his gun leading the way, Demo walked inside first while the rest of them followed. They were inside the kitchen and there were no lights to guide them. They moved slowly and cautiously, careful not to make any noise. They didn't know if Two was in the house alone, and they didn't want to alert anyone of their presence.

Once they made it to a hallway, they saw a light on in one of the rooms. Feez motioned for Poncho and Regal to see who was inside the room while the rest of the crew made their way down the hallway. Poncho and Regal stood on opposite sides of the doorway. Regal was the first to enter. A man sat in a chair with his back to the door. He didn't even see them coming. Regal pulled out his knife and swiped it across the man's neck in a single motion. Regal and Poncho both exited the room and joined the rest of the crew as they made their way through the house.

"Y'all, he got cameras in here," Shayla whispered, nodding her head up at the camera in the high corner of the room.

"He probably already knows we here, keep y'all head on a swivel," Feez instructed.

Nikki's heart raced, as the once easy sounding mission didn't seem so easy anymore. Gun in hand, she slowly walked between Feez and Regal as they turned the corner to go up the stairs. Two was still unseen but, for some reason, Nikki felt it wasn't the same for them. Nikki couldn't put her finger on it, but something felt off. Before she could say anything to the crew, she heard gunshots that sent Poncho tumbling down the stairs. The rest of the crew fired shots down the dark hallway and didn't stop until they heard the bodies drop. This was no longer a mission because the crew had walked right into an ambush.

"Shit, he's hit!" Nikki yelled as she ran back down the stairs towards Poncho. Feez wanted to follow her but he knew he had to complete the mission.

The rest of the crew continued down the hallway. Shayla pulled out a flashlight from her pocket and turned it on, shining the light down the hall in order to guide their way.

"Really Shay?" Demo looked over at her, shaking his head.

"What? The nigga already knows we here, so we might as well be able to see where the fuck we going."

"She got a point there," Feez chuckled.

"Poncho, are you okay?" Nikki asked as she examined his body, searching for blood that she didn't see.

Poncho moaned as he opened his eyes to see Nikki looking down on him. Rubbing his chest, Poncho took a deep breath before busting into laughter. Nikki looked at him like he was crazy, wondering why he was laughing after being shot.

"I knew my bulletproof vest would come in handy. And for some reason, something kept telling me to wear it today," Poncho stated.

Nikki smiled, happy that Poncho had followed his first mind. Helping him up from the floor, the two of them headed back up the stairs, joining the rest of the crew just as they were entering Two's room. As they walked in, they saw Two lying in bed under the covers.

"Ain't no fuckin' way he slept through all them gunshots," Shayla whispered.

"You right 'bout that, something ain't right 'bout this shit," Feez replied.

Demo slowly walked over to the bed and used his gun to shake Two. When he didn't move, Demo used his hand to roll him over. When Two's lifeless body hung halfway off the bed, the entire crew gasped.

"Someone already beat us to this shit, we gotta get the hell outta here," Feez informed.

"The niggas that was shooting at us was probably the ones that killed him," Shayla suggested.

"In real life, that's probably the truth," Nikki agreed.

"Come on, we gotta disable the cameras before we leave," Feez informed.

Shayla and Feez both ran out the room in search of the camera system while the rest of the crew made their way out the house. They all were back in the car within five minutes and began making their way back to their Airbnb.

"Was y'all able to erase the cameras?" Poncho asked.

"Shit, it was no need, somebody already did it," Shayla informed.

"Nigga, I'm glad yo ass is even still alive. I see yo ass had on that vest tonight. Yo ass got me ready to invest in a couple for me and Shay," Demo spoke.

"I been told you to get some, that shit saved my life tonight," Poncho replied.

"Y'all, what we gonna do? Should I call the client and let them know the job is done?" Feez asked, addressing the elephant in the room.

"Hell yeah, that nigga dead. It ain't our fault that he had a lot of people that wanted him dead. We came all the way here to do it. Done got shot at and shit. Hell, Poncho could have died. We gettin' paid for that shit," Shayla spoke.

The rest of the crew agreed with her, and Feez made the call to the client letting them know the mission was complete. When they got back to the Airbnb, everyone went to their rooms for the night. Nikki had just got out the shower when she heard a knock at her door. Still wrapped in her towel, she opened the door to see Feez on the other side.

"I was just coming to check on you," he announced.

Nikki smiled, opening her door wider and allowing Feez access. Feez walked in and was mesmerized by Nikki standing there in all of her natural beauty. There was no make-up, wigs or lashes, just pure flawless skin and wet curly hair. In Feez's eyes, she had never looked so beautiful. Without saying a word, Feez grabbed Nikki's face and kissed her passionately. Nikki didn't object as she allowed her tongue to dance with his.

Feez picked up Nikki effortlessly and carried her to the bed. He laid her down on the bed and gently unwrapped the towel from around her body. Taking one of her breasts into her mouth, he sucked hungrily as Nikki moaned softly. Feez placed gentle kisses from her breasts to her love box, allowing his tongue to taste her wetness. Nikki was in heaven as she grabbed Feez's head and grinded on his face. He allowed her to climax before he began to get undressed.

The moment Nikki felt Feez's stiff manhood enter her, she moaned so loudly, she was sure the rest of the house heard her. Feez stroked her slowly as he silenced her moans with soft wet kisses. If Nikki didn't know that Feez loved her before, she definitely knew it now. There was no way this was lust or just fucking, Nikki felt Feez's love with each stroke. Nikki fell asleep in Feez's arms, promising herself that she would tell him the truth about her when they made it back home.

CHAPTER FIFTEEN

akia woke up the next morning with a slight hangover. She and Simone had raided the minibar and got more than a little tipsy. Simone and the children were all still asleep, so Nakia took it upon herself to order them all breakfast. Once she was done, she went to check on Aden who was just waking up. Nakia had just got done feeding him when room service knocked on the door.

"Just a moment, I'm coming!" Nakia called out as she placed Aden in his playpen. Nakia walked to the door, opening it wide enough for the server to wheel in the tray of food.

"Nakia Pitchford, you are under arrest for failure to appear and obstruction of justice," Agent Scott announced as he began reading Nakia her rights.

"Fuck are you doing? What are you arresting me for? I

swear you sick in the head, you just want to cause me more problems," Nakia cried.

"I'm sorry Nakia, that is not my intentions. You were called by the State of Michigan to testify in court, and you failed to appear. This is not how I wanted this to work out."

Nakia called out to Simone, as the officers tried to walk her out of the hotel suite. Simone, hearing the desperation in Nakia's voice, ran out the room and towards her friend. Her jaw dropped when she saw two officers standing next to Nakia, who was in handcuffs.

"What the fuck is goin' on?" Simone asked, confused.

Special Agent Scott looked over at Simone and didn't say a word. She scoffed at his smugness before asking the question again. She didn't know why he was being so rude to her and not even answering her question. Agent Scott began walking out the suite while motioning the officers to follow him.

"Call Raphael and have him get me out!" Nakia managed to yell right before being forced out of the door. "You ain't shit! You the reason this shit is happenin' anyway. If you wouldn't have been tryin' to force me to testify, my fuckin' brother would still be alive. It wasn't enough for you to have my kids' uncle taken away from them, huh? You tryin' to take their mother too?"

Nakia was livid as she allowed the words to leave her lips freely. Nakia couldn't understand why Special Agent Scott was treating her like she was the criminal, when they already had the real criminal in custody. Nakia had never hated anyone in her life. She'd disliked people, not fucked with people but never hated anyone. However, her hatred for Agent Scott ran deep.

"Nakia, stop. Let's not try to act like this is anyone's fault but your own. All you had to do was testify, and this could have all been avoided. I'm done playing games with you; now, get in the car!" Special Agent Scott stated firmly.

"I just lost my brother because of this same man you want me to testify against. What the fuck do you think he's gonna do to me? Mannn, fuck you and the State of Michigan!"

The officers placed Nakia into the car, not giving a damn about her frustration. Nakia cried uncontrollably as she watched the car pull away from the hotel. She was officially under arrest, and that meant both her children and Simone were vulnerable. If the police could find her at the hotel, that meant Manny could too.

Simone rushed to her phone and called Raphael. His phone went to voicemail, and Simone left a message before calling right back. When Raphael didn't answer for the second time, Simone didn't know what to do.

"Auntie Simone, where did my mama go? Is everything okay?" Lexi asked, walking into the living room.

Simone knew Lexi heard everything that occurred and that she couldn't lie to her. So, instead, she just grabbed her and hugged her. Simone didn't know what to do next. All she knew was that she had the faces of Nakia's three children looking to her for their next move, and she couldn't let them down. There was a knock at the door that instantly startled Simone, causing her heart to skip a beat. She whispered for Lexi to go back into the room and waited for her get inside before Simone walked to the door slowly. She let out a long breath of ease when she heard the words *room service* being called out.

"Nakia must have ordered breakfast before the police came," Simone realized.

Opening the door, she allowed the woman to roll the tray inside the room. Food was the last thing on Simone's mind as she closed the door behind the server. Simone called the children to the living room to eat while she continued trying to get in touch with Raphael. There was no way Simone was going to let Nakia sit in jail. However, she also knew she couldn't take three children down to a police station.

"Fuck Raphael, answer the damn phone!" Simone spoke in frustration as she called him again.

RAPHAEL AND BLUE pulled up to Manny's southwest spot. They parked right in front of the house, not giving a damn about being seen. Their mind was on one thing only, and that was finding Rosa. The house was dark and seemed to be deserted, but they walked onto the porch anyway. They looked inside the windows to see if there was movement inside, but they saw nothing.

"I don't think anyone is here," Blue informed.

"Well, there's only one way to find out," Raphael replied, shooting the lock off the door and walking inside.

Blue was right behind him, gun raised, ready to shoot anything that moved towards them. They walked through the house, looking in every room and coming up empty. Not only was there no one inside the house, there was also nothing else inside either. No furniture, no work, no money, nothing. It was clear to the both of them that the house was abandoned.

"Are you sure this is his spot? It's nothing here," Blue asked.

"Yeah, this is his spot. Or was his spot. Let's get outta here, shit's a dead end."

The pair walked out as quickly as they'd walked in. Raphael grabbed his ringing phone as soon as they got inside the car, hoping it was Rosa. A frown of confusion spread across his face as he saw Simone's name flashing across his screen.

"What up doe?" Raphael answered.

"Oh, my God, Raphael, I've been trying to call you. Nakia got arrested. That special agent came up in here with two officers and took her to jail. I don't know what to do. The kids are asking me questions that I have no idea how to answer. Please Raphael, we need your help," Simone pleaded.

"Wait, slow down. What the hell do you mean they arrested Nakia? Arrested for what?" Raphael asked, trying to process the information he was being given.

"They arrested her for not coming to court and testifying in that trial. She wants you to come get her out and, if I were you, I would take a lawyer with you. That agent seemed like he was tough shit. The kids are fine, they heard everything though, so they been asking a lot of questions," Simone replied.

Raphael couldn't believe all this was going on at once. Here he was trying to find his sister, now he was worried about Nakia. *How the fuck did they even find out where Nakia was?* Raphael shook his head and informed Simone that he would meet his lawyer at the police station. Hanging up from Simone, Raphael quickly dialed his lawyer, letting him know he needed his assistance immediately.

"I'm on my way now, I'll see you there," his lawyer replied.

Raphael ended the call and began making his way to the police station with Blue riding shotgun. He knew he would have to change their hotel room now that their location had been compromised. Russell was well aware that if the police could find Nakia, then Manny could too. He had all the same resources the police did, if not more.

"Blue, the police got Nakia at the room this morning. Shit's gettin' real crazy. We gonna need to split up for a minute. I need you to go to the room and get Simone and the kids and take them to another one. Somewhere far out where no one will look for them. Put the room in your name so that it can't be traced back to them. Hit me after you do all that, and I'll tell you where I am," Raphael instructed.

Blue couldn't believe all this was going on either. *Why would Nakia, of all people, be in jail?* Blue thought. He had so many questions that he didn't ask. He knew Raphael had a lot on his plate, so he just nodded his head in agreement with the plan. They arrived at the police station about fifteen minutes later. Raphael spotted his lawyer the moment he pulled into the lot. He jumped out the car, leaving all his weapons inside and leaving the key fob in the driver's seat for Blue.

"Thanks for meeting me here, I don't know what's going on. Her best friend hit me and said she'd been arrested by an agent. I don't know what the hell is going on man. It's too much; from my parents being murdered, Rosa's missing and now Nakia. I need you to get her out, so she can be with our children," Raphael spoke.

"I heard about Fatbar and Harlin, but I was hoping it wasn't true."

"Yeah, it's sad but it's true," Raphael stated, hanging his head low.

"I'm sorry for your loss. Fatbar and Harlin were good people. Don't worry about yo girl, Raphael. I'm here now and you know Imma handle it. What's yo girl's name?" Kyree asked.

Kyree had been Raphael's family lawyer for the past ten years. Anytime there was trouble, Kyree was always there to get them out of it. Kyree was the only person that was not family who Raphael totally trusted.

"Nakia Pitchford," Raphael replied before following Kyree into the station.

Walking up to the desk, Kyree informed that he was there to post bail for his client. After giving the officer Nakia's name, Kyree watched her type it into her computer. Looking back to Kyree, she let him know that Nakia was being held without bail. Knowing that information, he asked to see Nakia, so he could better understand her case. The office led Kyree into the back and walked him to the room Nakia was being held in.

He walked inside the room to find Special Agent Scott speaking with Nakia. He knew then Nakia being arrested had something to do with Russell's trial. He knew he couldn't be Nakia's lawyer if this, in fact, did have something to do with his client; however, he wanted to see what he could find out.

"We are not going to send you to prison, Nakia; we just want you to testify. So, to ensure you do, you will be held here until the date in which you give your testimony," Special Agent Scott informed.

Did I just walk right into finding out who the high-profile witness of the case was? There is no way I can be this lucky.

"Special Agent, I think you would have to bring up charges in order to hold her here for more than seventy-two hours," Kyree stated.

"How did you get in here? I know you can't be her lawyer

because that would be a conflict of interest. Don't you think?" Special Agent Scott asked, looking at Kyree smugly.

Nakia looked over at Kyree, never seeing the man in her life. She didn't know who he was, let alone why he was in the room with them.

"Raphael sent me to check on you, Nakia; he's out in the waiting area," Kyree said.

Nakia smiled when she heard Raphael's name. It let her know that he was still out for her best interest. If Raphael had sent a lawyer, that meant he was the best at what he did. Nakia knew Raphael did big shit, so he for damn sure was going to have a good lawyer. She knew it would only be a matter of time before she walked out of there.

"I don't know who the hell Raphael is, Nakia, but you should really stay away from him. Nobody that really cares about you would have sent Russell's lawyer to see about you," Agent Scott revealed.

Nakia's mouth dropped open as she took in what Special Agent Scott had just told her. Just when she thought she could trust Raphael again, she realized she couldn't. *Why would he send him here? Raphael probably really is in on this shit for real. Could this nigga be trying to kill me now too?* Nakia knew then that she couldn't trust anyone around her.

Rosa laid on a cold concrete floor chained to iron pipes. She had no idea where she was or how she'd gotten there; however, she knew it wasn't good. The last thing she remembered was… she didn't remember what she was doing before she woke up. *Come on bitch, think; what the fuck were you doing?* Rosa racked her brain trying to remember what happened. Until, finally, she remembered being at the mall with Stretch. Sadness pierced her heart as she remembered the reason she'd went to the mall. *Shit, we had a shootout in the parking lot. Cash got shot and Stretch tried to get us away from... Manny,* Rosa remembered.

"Shit, Manny done got me."

"Where the fuck am I? I gotta figure out a way outta here before this crazy muthafucka kills me," Rosa told herself as she looked around the room for any clues as to where she was being held. However, there were none. Nothing was inside the room except her, the chains and the pipe she was chained to.

Rosa called out for help as she pulled and yanked on the chains, attempting to free herself. When nothing worked, she yelled out in defeat. It was clear to her that neither Stretch nor cash were with her because they would have already spoken up. She also knew that if Manny had her, it meant that Cash and Stretch were both dead.

"Fuuuucck!" Rosa yelled, knowing she had no way out. This was the end for her, and she hated that she would die in this cold dark basement all alone.

She heard the door open and loud footsteps coming down the steps. Rosa's heart beat fast because she knew the footsteps had to belong to Manny. There was nothing she could do. There was nowhere to run and no weapon to pull. So, as the strong woman she was, Rosa stood to her feet and awaited her fate. Surprise filled her when a man she didn't know stepped into her line of sight.

"Who the fuck are you?" Rosa asked, confused. She knew they had smoke with Manny and she expected to see him. However, the sight of a stranger made her feel even more uneasy.

"Probably the last new face you gonna see before you meet God," Javon answered. "It's a shame too, yo ass fine as hell. Imma need to get a taste of that shit before Manny kills yo ass," Javon continued.

Rosa recoiled, taken aback by Javon's statement. There was no way she was going to allow him to touch her, let alone taste anything she had. She eyed Javon as he walked closer to her, standing so close to her that she could smell the garlic on his breath. *This the muthafucka that was following us through the mall,* Rosa thought, remembering everything that happened. Javon ran his hand down her face and rested it around her neck without applying any pressure. It was something sexual about the way he touched her. When Javon rubbed the bulge in his pants against her thigh, Rosa thought she would throw up.

"Get the fuck off of me!" Rosa yelled as she jerked away from Javon.

Javon laughed sinisterly, pulling Rosa back towards him, this time applying pressure to her neck. "Bitch, you gonna learn the hard way that you ain't runnin' shit around here." Javon let Rosa go, pushing her down onto the concrete flooring. "I'm gonna have some fun with you and you don't even know it," Javon continued before walking away and going back up the stairs.

Rosa cried in fear as she prayed that she wouldn't be killed or raped. She knew Raphael was looking for her; however, she didn't even know where she was, so she knew he didn't.

"You gotta get the fuck outta here bitch. If you don't, you're gonna die," Rosa said aloud to herself. With nothing in the room to aid Rosa in doing that, she knew she would have to use her brain in order to survive.

"*B*itch, yo ass bout to stop workin', it's like yo stomach grew overnight. You got a pouch and shit now bitch," Tianna joked as she rubbed Tiny's stomach.

"Not this weekend bitch. I'm workin' all weekend, then I'll stop Monday. This gonna be a big money weekend, I can feel it," Tiny informed.

Tiny had plans with the money she was about to make over the weekend. She needed fifteen thousand dollars to have the full amount to hire the crew, and she was determined to get it. She hated the way her friend had been feeling lately, so she would be the one to do something to change it.

"Girl, we good on money. You know damn well we got a lot of that shit saved. If we need some more, this pussy is more than capable of making the money we need," Tianna said, grabbing a handful of her crouch.

"Bitch, I am not about to play with you," Tiny laughed before leaving the room to shower and prepare to work.

Both Tiny and Tianna worked well into the night, taking john after john. By the end of the night, they had twelve thousand dollars to split between the two of them. Tiny went back to her room feeling accomplished. She knew by Sunday, she would have all the money she needed and would be able to hire the crew.

Tianna let the hot water from the shower run down her body. It was the weekend, so she had until Monday morning to prepare herself to go back to Russell's trial. Tianna had thought she was over everything she'd went through with Russell; however, going to his trial had taken a lot out of her. Russell had lured her in with the promise of money. She was the one out there selling her pussy to different men every hour. Yet, she was giving him all of the money she was making.

The one time she decided she wanted to keep the money she made, Russell beat the hell outta her, forcing her to work all night to make him more money. Tianna cried as she reminisced. She wanted nothing more than for Russell to hurt the same way he'd hurt her. Even with the trial, Tianna was unsure if the judge's sentencing would be enough. Tianna couldn't help but to feel that prison was too good for Russell.

Even if the judge gave Russell life in prison, he would still have his life. That was not what Tianna wanted at all. Tianna wanted him dead; she needed him dead. Russell deserved to burn in hell for everything he'd done to her.

"I'm gonna kill that muthafucka," Tianna decided as she turned the shower water off.

Tianna laid down in bed and curled underneath her covers, promising herself that she was going gun shopping the next morning. She didn't care about any consequences at all. She'd already made it up in her mind that she would kill Russell, even if she didn't get away with it. Tianna would smile happily in that mugshot if it meant Russell would be in hell, never able to hurt another female again.

It was time for Tianna to fully take back her own life. She knew that would only start when Russell was no longer breathing. Tianna knew Russell well, so she knew that not even prison would stop Russell from hurting females. He would still be in prison running his sex trafficking ring from behind the wall, having all his girls putting their earnings on his books.

"Count yo days Russell, count yo muthafuckin days."

Feez and Nikki made it home that next morning safely and already paid from the mission. Feez had already wired the rest of the crew their cut of the money from the job. All he wanted to do was sit in front of his TV with a beer and watch the game. He showered and changed into a pair of grey sweat-pants and a white t-shirt before grabbing a beer from the fridge and heading to his living room.

Nikki, knowing it was time for her to come clean, walked

into the living room and took a seat across from Feez on the opposite couch. Her heart raced as she tried to figure out the words to say.

"Feez, I want to thank you for everything that you've done for me. And last night was truly amazing."

"It was amazing for me too. Jania, I really like you and I'm glad that you're here with me," Feez replied, standing up and sitting on the couch next to Nikki. "I want you to know that I'm for real about you. Last night wasn't just about no pussy for me," Feez continued.

"I'm for real about you too; that's why I need to talk to you about some things."

"You can talk to me about anything," Feez stated.

Nikki gave a half-smile as a single tear ran down her face. She was terrified to tell Feez her truth. Having him around had brought so much joy to her life, not to mention a new job and home. All she could do was pray Feez didn't kick her out after she told him everything.

"I have a lot to say. However, before I start, I want you to know that I never meant to lie to you. When I met you, I didn't think we would take it this far. But, now that we have, I need you to know the truth about me."

"I'm listening," Feez replied, and he truly was. Feez was giving her his undivided attention, ready to hear what she had to say.

"Feez, my name is not Jania, it's Nikki. Well, it's Nicole but I go by Nikki. I found a wallet in a gas station bathroom and the identification inside belonged to Jania Savage, I've been her ever since."

"Why take someone else's name? What's wrong with yours?" Feez asked, confused.

Nikki lowered her head, afraid that Feez would not like the answer to the question he'd just asked.

"I was wrapped up in some crazy shit about a year ago. I ended up gettin' away from that situation and things were good. That was until my homegirl was murdered inside our home and I ended up going on the run. I ended up gettin' in contact with a guy I knew, and he helped me out a lot, or so I thought. Turns out, he was just as horrible as the guy I was running from. When I found out I was pregnant, I knew I had to get away. I also knew the only way he would let me leave was if he was dead and couldn't stop me. So, I did what I had to do."

Feez looked at Nikki, grabbing her hand before he spoke, "I'm glad you told me the truth. Nikki, I don't ever want you to be scared to tell me anything. I want to build a relationship with you, and you and I need that to be built on pure honesty."

Nikki nodded her head in agreement as tears fell from her eyes. Feez wiped them away, letting her know there was no need to cry. It amazed Nikki how even after she lied to him, he was still gentle with her. She knew he was the type of man she needed in her life, and she hoped he never let her go.

"You said you got pregnant but never said what happened to the baby?" Feez asked.

Nikki had made it this far, so she knew she needed to go all the way. She was about to go in for the kill and could only pray that Feez would still want her after she told him. If he didn't, Nikki knew she couldn't be mad. If she was him, she wouldn't want her either with another man's baby inside of her.

"I'm pregnant now," she whispered. Nikki could see the words coming from her mouth like missiles as they hit him.

Feez dropped his head and shook it. He had so much to say, but the words wouldn't come out. He looked into Nikki's tear-filled eyes and his heart melted. He wanted to be there for her, to love her the way she deserved. However, he didn't truly know if he could do that while she was carrying another man's child. He wanted Nikki with him. He needed Nikki with him. It was something about Nikki that just made Feez feel better when he was with her.

"Is there anything else that you haven't told me? If so, now would be the time to let it out," Feez spoke.

"That's everything," Nikki replied. She contemplated telling him her real age but decided against it. She didn't feel a need to; her eighteenth birthday was just about a week away.

Feez nodded his head, believing what Nikki had told him. This was a lot to take in, and Feez needed time to process it all. He needed to think hard because he didn't want to make the wrong decision based off his emotions. "I need a minute," he said before motioning for Nikki to exit the room.

Nikki's heart dropped to her stomach as she feared that

Feez would not want to have anything else to do with her. Tears fell from her eyes as the thought of her past ruining her future was too much for her to handle. She didn't know what to do; she wanted to be with Feez. He'd given her a sense of security that she'd never had before. However, at the same time, she wouldn't beg him to allow her to stay.

Walking back into her room and closing the door behind her, Nikki grabbed her bags and began placing her belongings inside them. Tears clouded her sight as she wished she could rewind time. If she could, she would go back to before she caught feelings for Feez. She would have told him the truth about her and allowed him to make his own decision. Nikki couldn't believe how she'd just fucked up the one good thing that walked into her life.

Nikki was halfway through her packing when Feez knocked on the door. Quickly wiping her tears, Nikki answered the door. A look of confusion crossed Feez's face when he walked inside and found Nikki packing.

"You going somewhere?" Feez asked.

"Yeah, um… well, I thought… um… look, if you want me to leave now, I completely understand. I know I come with a lot and it's not your burden to carry. I just gotta pack my things, then I'll be gone."

"I never said I wanted you to leave." Feez walked up to Nikki and kissed her passionately. "I don't want you to go anywhere, I want you to stay right here with me. Do you want to leave?"

"No," Nikki whispered, placing kisses all over Feez's face and lips.

"Then, don't leave. We gonna be good, I promise. We gonna be a family and raise the baby together. Maybe even have some more kids. I'm in love with you, Ja… I mean Nikki and I don't want to let you go."

"I'm in love with you too, and I don't want to be with anyone but you. But, are you really ready for what you're asking for?"

Nikki wanted nothing more than to believe him and ride off into the sunset with him. However, Nikki had been fooled before and she didn't want that to happen again.

"Baby, I'm ready. I don't want nothing but you. So, I'm willing to take everything that comes with you. You said yo baby daddy is dead, right? You sure you killed him?"

"Yeah, I'm sure. That nigga dead, dead."

"Well, then, the baby will never have to know. Shit, nobody has to. It will be our baby with my last name," Feez suggested.

Feez had never been more serious in his life and wanted Nikki to know that. Feez had always wanted children and he wanted Nikki. So, if he could have them both in one wop, it would be a win/win for Feez.

"We need to make you a doctor's appointment first thing Monday morning. We need to make sure both you and the baby are good."

Nikki nodded her head in agreement. She knew she was

going on three months but had yet to see a doctor. For Feez to even suggest that showed Nikki that he was indeed serious.

The two of them sat on Nikki's bed and spoke about their plans for the future. Nikki cooked dinner for the two of them that night, and they both felt a love they had never experienced before. When she was done cooking, Nikki made their plates and walked them into the living room where they ate and watched the game together. It was that night that they became a couple. There was no more of Nikki sleeping inside the guest room. She moved herself and all her belongings into the master suite with Feez.

RUSSELL SAT in his cell with nothing but the thoughts in his head to keep him company. Fatbar turning state's witness on him had him feeling like nobody could be trusted. Fatbar had been like a father to him, teaching him everything he knew; now, he'd turned on him. There was no loyalty anymore, and Russell knew he had to do something. He didn't give a fuck if he was behind a wall; he was gonna make sure Fatbar got what he had coming. Kyree might not have thought Fatbar was the witness, but Russell knew he was. Russell couldn't think of any other reason Fatbar wouldn't be answering his calls.

Russell spent hours in his cell trying to come up with ways he could have Fatbar killed from behind the wall, until he was interrupted by a guard coming to his cell letting him know his lawyer was there to see him. *He must have some information about Fatbar for me,* Russell thought. Allowing the guard to place him in chains, Russell walked down the hall towards the visitation room. Kyree sat there with a smile on his face, and Russell knew he had good news.

"I know who the high-profile witness is," Kyree announced as soon as the guard left the room.

"Yeah, me too. I already told you it was Fatbar."

"And I told you it wasn't, and I was right. Fatbar is dead, and that's why you can't get in touch with him. Someone killed him and his wife in his home a couple of weeks ago. The witness is a woman named Nakia Pitchford. And get this, it's Raphael's girlfriend and the mother of his child."

"Damn, that's fucked up. I though he had turned on me. Who killed him?" Russell asked.

"I don't know. Fatbar was in a lot of shit. So, it could have been anyone."

"Hold up, you said the witness's name is Nakia Pitchford? Where does she work?" Russell asked.

"She used to work at the Courtyard Marriott from what I gathered while I was at the station. Isn't that where you almost got arrested at but jumped out the window? I'm sure that's why she's a witness. Do you remember talking to her at any point?"

"Yeah, I remember her. She's one of the original witnesses, remember? You gave me her and that white girl's name. Then, I called Fatbar to handle it. He clearly didn't handle shit because they are both still alive and testifying," Russell replied.

"Of course, Nakia is still alive. I just told you that Nakia is Raphael's girlfriend."

"Then he could have told me that. I gave him those names months ago. Way before he was murdered. He was supposed to handle that shit," Russell spoke.

Russell rubbed his hands over his head as he thought for a moment. Nothing made sense to him. *Raphael was there when I gave Fatbar the names of the witnesses, they said nothing to me about one of them being in their family. Man, what the fuck is going on?*

"I need you to really be on yo lawyer shit. Something ain't adding up and, when they start throwing stones at us, I need you to be right there with me duckin' them bitches."

CHAPTER SEVENTEEN

Nikki sat in her holding cell playing back Agent Scott's words in her head over and over again. *If he really cared about you, then why would he send Russell's lawyer to come see about you?* Nakia couldn't wait to speak with Raphael, so he could answer that same question. She wanted nothing more than to love Raphael, just as she did before any of this happened. However, it seemed that every day, her trust for him was being tested. She couldn't wait until she was released from jail and was finally able to talk to Raphael. It was clear that he knew way more than he was letting on.

Nakia wanted to be with Raphael and raise their family together. However, with the secrets he was keeping and the dangers that had come into her life since she met him, she didn't know if she could. Special Agent Scott told her she would have to testify either Monday or Tuesday, and Nakia didn't know how she was gonna sit in jail for that long. All she could think about was her children's safety. She prayed that Simone would be able to keep them safe until she could get to them. Until then, she could only wait until it was her time to testify.

Feez called the crew over to his house for Sunday dinner. He wanted to introduce Nikki to the crew as his woman while also letting them know that she would be going by her given name from here on out. Nikki had been in the kitchen for hours preparing everyone's favorite dishes, and Feez hoped it would be appreciated after they heard the truth. Nikki had an idea about how the crew would react to the bomb they were about to drop and could only hope that everyone would stay in good spirits.

Nikki listened to SWV tell someone how into them they were as she placed crab legs into a pot of boiling water. The door bell chimed, alerting them that someone had arrived, and that's when Nikki really started feeling nervous.

"Damn Jania, you got it smelling good as hell in here. What you cookin'?"

"Well, I wanted to make everyone's favorites, so it's lamb chops, crab legs, lobster, crab stuffed shrimp, twice baked potato salad, Caesar salad, baked and fried chicken, macaroni and cheese, collard greens, and ribs. I hope I got everything."

"Damn sis, who you feeding, an army?" Shayla joked.

"That's a lot of damn food, what's the occasion?" Shayla continued.

"I just wanted to cook. Me and Feez got some news for y'all and we wanted to share it over dinner."

"Ummm, okay," Shayla replied, eyeing the spread Nikki laid out.

"What up doe, y'all? Happy Sunday," Poncho greeted.

Once Regal arrived, they all headed into the dining room and took their seats at the table.

"Damn Jania, yo ass must have been cookin' all day?" Poncho asked.

"I just wanted us to enjoy a meal together. I didn't know what to cook, so I just cooked everyone's favorites."

Nikki was nervous for the crew to hear her secrets. She didn't know if they would be as accepting as Feez was. While Feez had assured her that everything would be okay, Nikki wasn't so sure.

"I don't know what had yo ass in the kitchen cookin' like this, but I'm glad it did," Regal beamed, placing a fork full of macaroni and cheese into his mouth.

Nikki was happy everyone liked her cooking; however, her heart skipped a beat when Feez announced they had something to talk to them about. *Damn, I at least thought he'd wait til dessert to let the cat out the bag. I guess it ain't no turning back now.*

"What's up? It's some money on the flow. Thanks for the meal and everything, but y'all ain't gotta butta me up to do no mission. I stay ready, so I ain't never gotta get ready," Poncho stated.

"Nah, this ain't bout no money, this family business," Feez assured.

"Everything good?" Shayla asked.

"Yeah, everything good with me. It's just a few things we wanna let y'all in on," Feez replied.

"Okay then, let it out then, nigga," Demo spoke.

Nikki sat there palms sweating, heart racing. She was so nervous that she thought she was gonna pass out. She knew this wasn't Feez's secret to tell, so she couldn't allow him to stand in the front line while she played the back. This was her doing, so she had to be the one to tell the crew.

"My name is not Jania, it's Nikki. I've been lying to all of you, including Feez. I truly apologize, I never meant for none of this to happen. I've been runnin' from some shit and I changed my name," Nikki announced, making her long story short.

"What? Fuck you mean yo name ain't Jania? Feez, what the fuck is this shit? We done let her all in the crew, lettin' her know all of our business and we don't even know who the fuck she is," Regal stated.

They had gone years without letting any new members in, and everything was going smooth. They knew they could trust one another to have the other's back. They'd taken that oath in middle school. Here they were letting in a new face and she turned out to be a liar.

"She could be the opps, what if someone sent her to get at us? What if she the fuckin' police?" Regal continued before standing from his seat and walking out of the dining room.

The remaining members of the crew looked over at her, waiting for her to answer. The way she just came in and became part of the crew so fast had everyone thinking the same thing.

"I'm not the police, nor was I sent by anyone. I simply ran into some problems and had to change my name so that I wouldn't be found," Nikki assured.

"Look y'all, Nikki is my girl now. If y'all respect me, then y'all will respect her. If I don't have a problem with what's going on, then y'all shouldn't either," Feez spoke.

"Ooh, so, now y'all coming out in the open, I already knew. I called that shit the other day. Didn't I Jania… I mean Nikki? Damn, it's gonna take me some time to get used to that. But, long as Feez is happy, then I'm good," Shayla replied.

"Yeah, me too. Fuck all the bullshit; she was runnin' from someone and she ain't know us. Now, she do, so she tellin' us the truth. No harm, no foul. Don't pay Regal no mind, that nigga just paranoid. He will be cool once he calms down," Demo assured.

Nikki nodded her head. She understood Regal's doubt; she just wished he would have stayed and listened to her. She wanted the whole crew to understand that she was only doing what she had to do at the time. She wasn't there to attack the crew; she wanted to be a part of it.

"I don't give a fuck 'bout none of that shit. Can I get some more butter for my crab legs?" Poncho spoke with a mouth full of food.

"Yo big hungry ass. The entire world could be burning down and, as long as you had food, yo ass would be okay," Shayla joked.

Thy all busted out laughing knowing Shayla's statement was true. Feez walked around the table and grabbed Nikki's hand, giving her a look that said *I told you everything would be okay.* Nikki smiled back at Feez before lying her head on his shoulder.

"Is anyone gonna go get Regal?" Shayla asked.

"Nah, just let him blow steam for a minute. He will be good when he calms down," Demo replied.

"We have some more news for y'all," Feez announced, this time with a smile.

"Damn, can y'all chill with the bomb dropping for a minute? I'm still processin' the fact that I gotta call her Nikki now," Demo stated, pointing at Nikki.

"This is a good bomb, I promise," Feez spoke.

Before he could say anything else, the landline rang. They all looked at each other, knowing the ringing phone meant another mission. Feez walked over and answered it. After listening to the caller speak for several seconds, Feez announced that the crew would be available.

"Cool, wire half now and we will leave tomorrow morning," Feez spoke before hanging up the phone.

"What's the next mission?" Poncho asked.

"We hittin' Detroit tomorrow, some dude named Russell. This gonna be a different kinda mission though. This nigga is in jail and on trial right now."

"On trial? So, we gotta kill a nigga in front of the police?" Demo asked, confused.

"Yeah, but shit's gonna be cool. All we gotta do is get him while they either bringing him in or out of court. I'll get on Google maps and check the location to get a layout of the area. I'll have our plan ready by tomorrow morning," Feez assured.

Feez looked over to Nikki as she fell into her chair. Her skin was pale and clammy, and she looked like she'd just saw a ghost. Feez rushed over to her and knelt down beside her, wrapping his arms around her tightly. He didn't know what just happened, but he wanted her to know that he was right by her side.

"Baby, are you okay?" Feez whispered.

"Russell, that's the nigga I been runnin' from. I hate that nigga! I gotta be the one that pulls that trigga y'all," Nikki spoke, looking up at them through tear-filled eyes.

"Are you sure it's the same person?" Feez asked.

"I'm gonna take a look at the picture when they send it to you, but I'm almost certain it's him," Nikki replied. "That nigga did a lot of bad shit to a lot of females, including me. If this is him, then I can't wait to be his fuckin' karma."

"If it's him, then you can't go at all. If he sees you, that might blow our cover and we can't have that. We already gonna be hot as fuck, doin' that shit in front of the courthouse; we don't need nothing else to worry about," Poncho stated.

Tears flowed down Nikki's face at the mere mention of Russell's name. She needed whoever hired them to send the photo quicky, so she could see it. If it in fact was Russell, nothing no one could say would stop Nikki from pulling that trigger. He'd caused her so much hurt that only his death would bring her joy.

"Nikki, what did this Russell dude do to you? Why can't we just go and kill him for you if it is him? You still will get a cut of the money either way if that's what you worried about. You not gonna lose money if you sit this one out," Shayla informed.

Nikki spent the next fifteen minutes breaking down her life story to the crew. She told them how she was living at home with her crackhead mother. How Russell lured her to Detroit with the promise of money and a better life. By the time she was done, everyone in the room was ready to kill Russell for free because of the way he treated Nikki. The phone rang again, and Feez was informed that the picture of Russell had been sent.

"Is this him?" Feez asked, showing Nikki the photo.

"Yeah, that's that sex traffickin' muthafucka right there. Y'all gotta let me get at this nigga; this shit is personal."

. . .

TINY FELT ACCOMPLISHED after hiring the crew. She wanted to tell Tianna what she'd done; however, Tiny decided to wait until the job was finished. She couldn't wait to see the look on her friend's face when she told her Russell was dead. Tianna had been her rock since they had escaped the brothel. With the father of her child being murdered, Tianna was all Tiny had. So, she knew they had to look out for one another. This was Tiny's way of doing that.

Tiny only had five thousand dollars left after hiring the crew, but she was okay with that. She knew they would all be okay. Even though Tiny would not be working for the next few months, she knew that Tianna would make sure they were good, same as she would do if the shoe was on the other foot.

Heading to the kitchen, Tiny prepared somewhat of a pre-celebration dinner for the two of them while Tianna was out. After seasoning the steaks, Tiny turned on her phone and allowed her Apple music app to play through her wireless speaker.

"Oh, you in here cookin', cookin' huh?" Tianna asked, walking inside the kitchen.

"I'm just making some surf and turf with potatoes and salad, nothing big. Dinner will be ready in a few."

"Good, I'm starving, and you got it smelling good as hell in here. Imma go take a shower and I'll be back in a minute."

Once Tianna was in her room, she took the gun she'd just purchased and placed it inside her nightstand. She'd just purchased the gun that she was going to kill Russell with and she had never felt so liberated. She didn't know how she was gonna kill Russell. She also knew there was no way she was going to be able to take a gun inside the courtroom with her. However, she knew she was going to do it, so the when would come soon enough.

"I hope that nigga sees my face before he goes to hell."

Rosa sat in the cold dark basement mouth dry and stomach growling. She'd had nothing except a bottled water and a pack of crackers since she'd gotten there. She was becoming delusional from the lack of sleep; however, she was afraid to close her eyes even for a second, out of fear that she would either be murdered or raped in her sleep. She was unsure how long she'd been down there because there were no windows in the basement. However, Javon had been down to see her twice since the first time she'd gotten there, and every time he had on different clothes. So, she estimated she'd been down there for at least two days.

The door opened, and she heard the footsteps coming down the stairs. Rosa knew it was Javon, and she hoped he had some food and water for her. Shock was all over Rosa's face when she saw Manny appear in front of her.

"You look like you just saw a ghost," Manny spoke.

So many emotions ran through Rosa's head at once. She was both angry and hurt all at the same time. She was looking into the eyes of the man that killed both of her parents and her man. She wanted to kill him, but she couldn't even get to him. There wasn't much she could do while she was chained to pipes. She knew she would have to play things smart because Manny had the upper hand.

"Don't you think you've done enough? You killed mama and daddy, your aunt and uncle. They raised you and treated you like you were their own child. But I guess that ain't mean shit to you, huh?" Rosa replied.

Rosa's eyes burned and tears threatened to fall from her eyes as she spoke about her parents. She hated him for what he'd done to her life. The way he'd just turned her world upside down without even a second thought. Rosa was just the happiest she'd ever been and, in a split second, it was all taken away from her by Manny's hands.

"I haven't done enough. You standin' here cryin' bout yo parents when yo parents had my brotha killed. Their own fuckin' nephew, someone they raised like their own son. If they would have done that to yo brotha, what would you do?" Manny replied, walking closer to Rosa.

"If you think my parents had anything to do with Niko's death, then you out yo fuckin' mind. They loved Niko, you know that shit just as well as I do."

"You gonna say whatever you think you gotta say in order to save yo life. Thing is, I don't want to kill you. You the only one I know for sure didn't have anything to do with shit. You not even in this life, never have been. But don't get shit twisted, I will kill yo ass if I have to," Manny spoke honestly.

"Then, Manny, why am I here? If you don't wanna kill me

and know I didn't have anything to do with this, then why do you have me here chained the fuck up?"

"Because if it's one thing I know, it's that Raphael will come and get you. Now, he can either bring me his bitch and come get you, or he can keep his bitch and allow his sister to die. Now, call him, so we can see the choice he makes," Manny ordered, holding his phone out for her to take.

Raphael and Blue had been looking for Rosa nonstop for the past two days. They had only gotten a few hours of sleep, knowing that every moment spent not looking for Rosa was a moment wasted. All they wanted to do was bring Rosa home safely, and even that sounded like too much to ask for.

"What's next OG? We've been a lot of places and we still haven't found Rosa. We don't even have no leads on where she might be," Blue stated, looking to Raphael for their next move.

Raphael, however, was just as lost as Blue. The fear of never finding his sister plagued him. His phone rang, jogging him out of his thoughts. He looked down at his screen to see a number that he didn't recognize. Raphael started not to answer the call but swiped talk at the last second. His eyes widened when he heard Manny's voice on the other end. Raphael listened to Manny tell him how he had to choose between his sister and his son's mother.

"What's the address?" Raphael asked.

Manny spoke into the phone, giving Raphael his location. Manny informed Raphael that if he did not bring Nakia with him and trade her off for Rosa, Rosa would die. Manny was sick of the back-and-forth shit. He was ready to get this shit over and done with.

"You happy now? You bout to get yo wish and get both Raphael and Nakia. You're gonna kill them just like you did my parents and Jalyn," Rosa spoke.

"No, Imma kill them like they killed Niko."

Twenty minutes later, Raphael and Blue pulled up to a home on the east side that neither of them had seen before. It was do or die, and they were both ready to kill Manny. They both made sure they were well strapped before they exited the car. Raphael motioned for Blue to go around the back while he went in through the front. They didn't know exactly what they were walking into, so they made sure to keep their heads on a swivel.

Once inside, Raphael heard Rosa's voice instantly. She was arguing with someone that he assumed to be Manny. Following the sound of her voice, Raphael stopped at the top of a set of stairs that looked to lead to a basement.

"She's down there," Raphael whispered to Blue when he appeared just a short moment later.

Raphael was just a few steps away from getting his sister back and killing Manny at the same time. His trigger finger itched as he anticipated shooting holes into Manny. Both Raphael and Blue wasted no time walking down the stairs gun first. It was time to bring Rosa back home and stop this war. Too many people had died because of it, and Raphael knew

Manny would be the last to die. Manny, being taken off guard, could not draw his gun fast enough before he felt the cold steel of Blue's gun against his head.

Raphael rushed over to Rosa, looking at her chained to a damn pipe like a pit-bull puppy. Anger shot up through his bones as he saw the state his sister was in. Shooting the lock from the chain, the chain fell to the ground, releasing Rosa from its hold. Rosa instantly stood to her feet and hugged her brother, happy that she'd been rescued.

"Y'all really think shit's gonna be that easy, huh?" Manny asked, Blue's gun still pressed against his head.

"Shit looks easy as hell to me," Blue replied.

Raphael was just about to walk Rosa out to the car when Javon walked down the stairs. Seeing Blue with Manny at gunpoint caused Javon to draw his weapon, firing several shots in their direction. In the split second it took for Blue's head to turn, Javon had shot him, causing Blue to drop to the ground and allowing Manny to break free. Manny quickly pulled his pistol before shooting Blue again and turning to Raphael. They both stood there, guns aimed at one another ready to fire. Looking down to see Blue lying on the floor bleeding out, Raphael shot at the same time Manny did, sending them both dropping to the floor.

CHAPTER EIGHTEEN

"Okay, Nakia, it looks like today will be the last day of trial. So, this will be the day you testify," Special Agent Scott announced, walking into Nakia's holding cell.

He handed Nakia a garment bag with a black suit inside before informing her that he would be back shortly to escort her to the bathroom to dress. Nakia didn't say a word as she took the bag and sat back down on her cot. She would be happy when all this was over, so she could get back to her children. She knew they missed her just as much as she missed them. *They probably over there driving Simone up a wall with questions about where I am,* Nakia chuckled to herself.

"Once you're dressed, Detective Mallory will be here to escort you to court. She will also be briefing you on your testimony," Agent Scott continued.

When Nakia failed to answer him for a second time, he nodded his head and walked away. There was no need for any extra word; he'd done what he'd set out to do and, that was bring Nakia in to testify. Between Nakia's testimony and the testimony of the high-profile witness, Agent Scott knew they had the case in the bag. There was no way Russell would walk out of that courtroom without a guilty verdict.

Once Nakia showered and dressed, Detective Mallory arrived to escort her to court. Nakia though about making a run for it but quickly decided against it. Figuring that just going to testify and getting it over with would be less painful than being on the run. She walked into the courthouse and followed Detective Mallory to the courtroom.

The crew made their way onto the privet jet, ready to take the flight to Detroit. After the crew heard Nikki's story, they decided to go against their rules and allow Nikki to come on the mission. Feez, who'd scoped out the area via Google maps, had come up with an airtight plan. They all knew that a shooting at a courthouse in front of police would cause the entire city to go into lockdown. So, they wanted to make sure they were on their way out of Detroit as soon as the job was done.

After checking into the Airbnb, they all changed their clothes and grabbed their guns before heading right back out. They didn't know when Russell would be entering or exiting the court; however, they all knew those would be the only times they would have a chance at completing their mission.

Demo and Shayla would sit in an SUV parked a few hundred feet from the courthouse. Regal, dressed in an all-black suit, walked inside the courtroom. He would be the one to give the signal to them once court was adjourned while Poncho, Feez and Nikki would be staked out on the roof of an old high-rise across the street. Their plan was foolproof. The only one of them that would ever be seen was Regal. However, he looked so different from his regular self, even if he was seen again, no one would recognize him. His low cut Caesar had been replaced with a male frontal that was braided straight to the back. His once smooth face had been spray painted with black hairspray into the shape of a goatee.

Regal would be the one to sit inside the courtroom and listen to everything Russell had done to Nikki. Feez did that intentionally, so Regal could see things from Nikki's point of view. He hoped that once Regal found out everything, he would see why Nikki changed her name. Feez needed for the entire crew to get along with Nikki. She was a part of the crew and she was also his woman now, so he needed Regal to forgive her.

Tianna made her way inside the courtroom with a huge smile on her face. She knew today was the day she would kill Russell. Tianna had rented a car the day before simply so she could drive herself to court the next morning. She'd concealed her pistol inside the armrest of the rental, planning to retrieve it right before the officers walked Russell out of the building.

In all honesty, Tianna didn't give a fuck about being

caught. She was not a killer by any means. However, Russell had pushed her, so it had to be done. Russell had beaten, raped, and sent her to Albania without any remorse. So, there would be no remorse when she killed him. Tianna didn't give a damn if she died right beside Russell, as long as she took him out first.

Tianna walked into the courtroom and sat in the back closest to the door. She needed to be the first person out of the courtroom, so she could make it to her car before they took Russell out of the building. She watched, as the prosecution called their first witness to the stand.

"Ms. Pitchford, can you tell me your place of employment approximately one year ago?" the prosecutor asked.

"Yes, around that time, I was employed at the Courtyard Marriott."

"And is that the one located at DTW?"

"Yes, that is correct," Nakia replied.

The prosecutor went on to question Nakia about the events that led her to call the police until he rested. At that moment, Kyree stood to his feet, walked to the front of the courtroom and began questioning Nakia. Her heart dropped as she looked into his eyes. She knew then Special Agent Scott was telling the truth about him, and he really was Russell's lawyer. *Why the fuck would Raphael send Russell's lawyer to come check on me?*

"Ms. Pitchford, have you ever seen my client with any

female while he stayed at your place of employment?" Kyree asked.

"No, I did not," Nakia answered truthfully.

"Then, how do you know he was with young girls as you stated in your original statement?"

"Because he told me he was with them. Your client told me he was in a poly-relationship with two young girls. He said it worked out for him because they were really young."

"Young could have meant anything. What made you assume they were underage if you didn't even see them with my client?" Kyree asked.

"I didn't assume anything. Their birth dates proved they were underage, not my assumptions," Nakia shot back.

"Objection, he is badgering the witness!" the prosecutor yelled as he stood to his feet.

"No need, I'll retract," Kyree stated.

Kyree went on questioning Nakia, and her blood boiled with each question. Nakia felt Kyree was calling her a liar when he was the one defending a sex trafficking killer. On top of that, he'd tried to come see Nakia as her attorney, knowing it was a conflict of interest. It felt like forever but, soon, Nakia was able to step down from the stand. It was at that time the prosecution called their high-profile witness to the stand.

"I though Nakia was the high-profile witness?" Russell whispered to Kyree.

"I did too," he replied.

"Man, who the fuck is it?"

Kyree didn't say a word, only shook his head, still not knowing who the high-profile witness was. When the witness finally took the stand, both Russell and Kyree could not believe their eyes. Russell tried to keep his composure but, at that point, he no longer cared. He knew he would be going to jail and, if he had to go, he would be taking everyone with him.

"You disloyal muthafucka! You really 'bout to come in a fuckin' courtroom and testify against me?" Russell yelled, hurt and anger pultruding from his voice.

"Order in the courtroom! Order! Defense, you better get your client under control, or it won't be good for him," the judge ordered.

Russell didn't give a damn about what the judge said. He needed answers and he needed them now. Never in a million years did he think of his own brother being the high-profile witness; it never crossed his mind. It hurt him to think it was Fatbar; however, the fact that it was his brother, his blood brother, crushed him.

Travis took his seat and began answering the questions under oath. He couldn't look Russell in his eyes because he knew what he was doing was wrong. If the shoe was on the other foot, Russell would have died before turning state's witness on him. Now, here Travis was sitting on the stand, prepared to give the testimony that would put his own brother behind a wall for a very long time.

"You are the defendant's brother, correct?" the prosecutor asked.

"Yes, that is correct. We were raised together our entire lives."

"Do you know the minors in question?"

"Yes, I do, they worked for Russell," Travis replied.

"When you say worked for him, what do you mean by that?"

"Russell ran a prostitution business from his phone. He set up a website that men would order women from. Russell would accompany the females to see the men, where they would then exchange sexual favors for money," Travis revealed.

"Have you ever witnessed the defendant in the middle of said exchange?"

"Yes, I have."

"These females that worked for your brother, were they women or minors?" the prosecutor asked.

"They were minors. Russell liked to get the young girls, so he could mold then into who he wanted them to be."

"And you've witnessed this with your own eyes?"

"Yes, several times," Travis responded.

The prosecutor spent the next fifteen minutes questioning Travis, and he told it all. The part he played in all of this disgusted him, and this was his way of righting his wrongs. He hated the fact that he had to snitch on his brother. However, the thought of the part he played in ruining those young girls' lives was eating at him. Travis didn't care about getting any time taken off of his sentence. He knew he deserved to go to jail; however, he needed to do the right thing before doing so.

Once the prosecutor was done questioning Travis, it was Kyree's turn. Kyree didn't even want to stand up. He'd known once he saw Travis take the stand that they'd lost the case. So, instead of questioning him, Kyree rested, letting the court know he had no questions for the witness. Travis was told to step off the stand while both the defense and prosecution went into their closing statements.

"The jury just went in for deliberation," Regal spoke into his earpiece as he walked into the bathroom.

"That shit could take hours. Hell, even days," Shayla said.

They were all hooked up to the same channel. This was so everyone would know what's going on and when to be ready to aim.

"Nah, I think his shit gonna be quick. That nigga that's on trial is a fuckin' monster. They giving him time for sure. Even his brother came to testify against him," Regal announced.

"Wait, Travis testified?" Nikki asked, shock evident in her voice.

"Yes, he just got off the stand right before they went in for deliberation. Yo, Nikki, I need to apologize to you. I had no idea what you went through until I listened to the shit that nigga did. I see why you changed yo name and went on the run now," Regal continued.

"Thank you, Regal, your apology means a lot to me."

It only took the jury all of thirty minutes to agree on a verdict. Everyone reentered the courtroom, ready to hear what the foreman had to say. The entire courtroom cheered when the foreman announced the guilty verdict. Tianna watched, as Russell just shook his head. The judge announced a sentencing date that was a month away before adjourning court. Tianna was the first one out the door, ready to head to her car. It was go time, and she was gonna make sure she stood on business.

"He's about to walk out the courtroom now; y'all get ready," Regal spoke.

Nikki's heart raced as she began setting up her sniper riffle, aiming it directly at the doors of the courthouse. She was ready to double tap her trigger. She knew that all of her stress and baggage would be lifted once Russell was dead. She saw the doors open and watched as a few officers walked out first. When she saw Russell step outside in chains, her heart dropped. It was the first time in over a year that she'd seen his face. Anger shot through her body as she began playing out horrible memories in her head. She aimed for his head but, before she could pull her trigger, she saw Russell fall to the ground.

"It's a shooter!" one of the officers yelled.

"Come on y'all, we gotta go!" Feez called out as they grabbed their guns and began running down the stairs of the building.

"I didn't shoot him though. Who the fuck shot him?" Nikki yelled out.

"What do you mean you didn't shoot him? I saw that nigga fall," Poncho asked.

"I saw him fall too, but I never pulled the trigger so that means it was another shooter," Nikki reiterated.

Feez looked over at Nikki, stunned by her revelation. The three of them ran down several flights of stairs before running out of the back door and down an alley, meeting up at the SUV Demo and Shayla sat in. The three of them got in and they all pulled off down the street, headed back to the Airbnb.

"Who the fuck shot him?" Poncho asked, breathing heavily from running.

"Fuck you mean who shot him? Feez, you hit?" Demo asked, looking at Feez through his rearview mirror.

"Nah, not me, we talkin' 'bout the hit. Nikki was ready to fire when before she did, someone else shot the target," Feez uttered.

"What? Something is going on. Our last too missions had others there to hit the target; what are the odds of that shit?" Shayla asked, fearing something sinister was taking place. "What if someone is tryin' to set us up?" she continued.

Shayla couldn't help but to feel their last two jobs were connected. The fact that both times someone else was there to kill their target didn't sit right with her. *What if this was a set up to get us caught?* As she thought more and more, she knew how strange it was for someone to be asked to commit a murder in front of the police. They were the best in the business and, if anyone could do it, they could. However,

Shayla couldn't help but feel like something was about to go wrong.

"I don't think the two are connected in any way. Both of them were fucked up, so anyone could have wanted either of them dead," Feez suggested.

Nikki knew that Russell had a lot of enemies, so it didn't surprise her that more than one person wanted him dead. She didn't know who called in the crew, but she had a feeling it was one of the females that use to work for Russell. He treated all his women horribly, so Nikki knew they all wanted him dead. *Shit, if I wasn't with the crew, I would probably be outside the courts shootin' his ass too*, Nikki thought to herself.

"Feez is right. I'm sure everyone wanted Russell dead. I know I did," Nikki reported.

The crew all met up at the Airbnb and gathered their things, headed straight to the private jet. The shooting of Russell was on every news and radio station in Michigan and the surrounding areas. At the moment, they had no leads; however, none of the crew wanted to stay around and find out otherwise.

Tianna walked into her house both nervous and happy. She'd killed Russell just as she'd set out to do. Walking into her room, she immediately got into the shower. She now had blood on her hands and hoped the shower would wash it off. Although she was happy about what she'd done, she couldn't help the paranoia. *What if someone saw me? Would they be able to point me out?* She knew she couldn't tell anyone what she did and, soon, she would be letting Tiny know they would be moving out of Michigan. There was no way she would stay there after shooting Russell dead in front of the court.

Once Tianna was out the shower and in clean clothes, she went downstairs where Tiny was in the kitchen about to cook dinner. Tianna tried to hide her nervousness as she entered but knew it was all over her face. Tiny, however, seemed to be in good spirits as she handed Tianna a drink once she walked in.

"Heyyyy, bitch, turn up that music and have a drink. We celebrating tonight," Tiny announced.

"What are we celebrating?" Tianna asked, confused. She was thankful for the drink because she definitely needed it.

"We gotta toast it up bitch," Tiny exclaimed, holding her glass in the air.

"Umm, first off, what are you drinking? Yo pregnant ass bet not have no liquor in that glass. And what are we toasting to?"

"Girl, no, you got a cranberry and vodka. I just have cranberry juice with a lime, to make it look fancy," Tiny laughed. "And, bitch, I did something that I know you would appreciate. So tonight, we're toasting to Russell's death," Tiny announced as she held her glass up.

Tianna almost fell over when she heard those words. *How the fuck did she know Russell was dead? Did someone tell her? If she knew, that meant someone saw me. I gotta get the fuck outta here tonight,* Tianna thought.

"What are you talking about?" Tianna asked.

She wanted to play it cool and not let on that she'd done anything. As long as the police didn't come knocking at her door before she had a chance to leave, this was a secret Tianna would be taking to her grave.

"I hired the crew to kill Russell, and they did that shit because it's been all over the news. You must have left court before it happened, but that nigga is dead. And I'm the one that made that shit happen. I saw how much you were hurt by what you did. I know what we went through in Albania. I couldn't find the nigga that put me there, but we knew exactly where Russell was. I had to do something," Tiny stated.

Tianna was taken aback by what Tiny was telling her. Placing the glass to her lips, she took a huge gulp before she replied, "Who is the crew and what do you mean you hired them?"

"The crew is a group of assassins, the best in the business, and I hired them to kill Russell for you," Tiny replied. "Why you lookin' like that? I though you would be happier than this. Did you just hear me say that nigga was dead?" Tiny reiterated.

Tianna just stood there confused. Here, Tiny was telling her that she'd hired some assassins to kill Russell when she knew she was the one who pulled the trigger. If she hired them, that meant she paid them, and it was for a job they didn't do.

"Tiny, how much did you pay these people?" Tianna asked frantically.

"It don't matter what I paid, just know that nigga is no longer. He can never hurt you again. You don't have to worry about that nigga getting out and hurting you again. Bitch, I thought you would be happier than this," Tiny recoiled, not understanding the way her friend was responding to the news. *Why the fuck is she so worried about the cost when I just told her the nigga that hurt her is dead?*

"Tiny, just please tell me how much money you gave them people?" Tianna pleaded, knowing Tiny had wasted money that they would now need.

"Damn, bitch, calm down. I gave them eighty thousand. Which, if you ask me, was a small price to pay to assure Russell never hurt you again."

"Tiny, you spent that money for nothing. The crew or whoever you hired didn't kill Russell, I did," Tianna revealed. "We gotta find out how to get yo money back. We gonna need it, so we can leave Michigan like tomorrow."

Tiny didn't know what to say. She'd thought she was doing a service for her friend, only to find out her friend already had everything covered. Tiny ran to her phone, calling the crew immediately. When they didn't answer, she began to get nervous. Eighty thousand dollars was a huge amount to spend on nothing, and Tiny hoped she'd not been played.

Nakia didn't make it out of court until three hours after the trial had ended. She was just about to be escorted back to the police station so she could be released when Russell was shot. Once she was finally free, the first thing she did was call Simone, so she could locate her children. It had been days since Nakia saw them, and she missed them tremendously.

After ordering an Uber, Nakia made it to their hotel about forty-five minutes later and rushed up to the penthouse. When Simone opened the door holding Aden, Nakia grabbed him and placed several kisses onto his forehead.

"Mama missed you so much, baby boy."

Hearing Nakia's voice, Rashaud and Lexi ran into the living room, greeting their mother with their smiling faces. They ran to her, hugging her tightly. Nakia's heart was overjoyed as she reunited with her children. At that moment, nothing else mattered. Not Russell, not that case, not Manny or the war between the families. Right then and there, the only thing that mattered to Nakia was her children. Nakia vowed to them that she would never leave them again.

Nakia's phone rang, and she ignored it as she listened to her children tell her what they'd done the few days Nakia was away. When her phone rang for the third time in a row, Nakia decided she should answer it, fearing that whoever was calling her had important news. Answering her phone, Nakia was surprised to hear Rosa's frantic voice on the other end.

"Nakia, Raphael's been shot! We at Harper hospital!" Rosa yelled into the phone.

Hearing the words made Nakia lightheaded and she almost passed out. Raphael was hurt and he needed her. Nakia looked over to Simone with tear-filled eyes, and Simone knew something was wrong.

"Come on y'all, let's go play a game while mommy's on the phone," Simone suggested, taking Aden from Nakia and walking the children back to a separate room, returning several moments later.

"Nakia, what's going on? Simone asked, walking back into the room.

"I gotta go, I just ordered an Uber. Raphael is in the hospital, he's been shot."

EPILOGUE

Six months later

Nikki laid in bed cuddled up next to Feez as they watched the flames from the fireplace dance. This was about to be Nikki's first real Christmas with loved ones to share it with, and she couldn't have been more excited. She'd spent days decorating the house, with each room having its own Christmas tree and color theme. Nikki was nine months pregnant and, although Feez had informed her that he would have Christmas dinner catered, she insisted on cooking.

"Are you happy, baby?" Feez asked, whispering into Nikki's ear.

"I'm beyond happy baby, I'm ecstatic. I've never had anything like this before. I thank God every day for bringing you into my life," Nikki revealed, rolling over to kiss Feez on the lips.

"I'm so in love with you, Nikki."

"I'm in love with you too but, most of all, I gotta pee," Nikki laughed.

"Then, take yo pissy ass in the bathroom then," Feez joked.

Nikki laughed while flipping the covers off of her and standing to her feet. She felt the pressure in the bottom of her stomach as liquid poured from between her legs. She looked up at Feez to see him looking down at the floor.

"Oh, my God, I think…"

"Yo water broke," Feez said frantically, finishing Nikki's sentence.

Jumping up from the bed, Feez rushed around the room, gathering clothes for them to put on. It was time; Nikki was in labor and he had to get her to the hospital. Once they were dressed, Feez grabbed Nikki's hospital bag and helped her to the car. Feez called Demo from the car, letting him know Nikki was in labor. Demo informed him that he would contact the rest of the crew and meet them at the hospital.

Nikki had no idea how much labor hurt until she was lying in a hospital bed with Feez on one side and Shayla on the other. They were both holding her legs back, coaching her to push while she felt her entire vagina was being ripped out from the inside. She screamed and pushed for the next three hours and, by the time it was over, Nikki was exhausted. However, when the doctor laid her beautiful baby girl onto her chest, everything was worth it. All the pain Nikki had gone through, all the hurt and horrible decisions had led her right here. She looked up into Feez's eyes and felt a love so unconditional that nothing could break it.

"I want to name her Blessing," Nikki whispered.

Tianna walked into the main entrance of Southern Regional hospital to pick up Tiny and the baby. They were being released, and Tianna had spent all night cleaning and getting the house prepared for the new baby. She wanted to make sure everything was perfect for them. She'd already knew he would be a stubborn child, staying in Tiny three weeks past his due date. The doctors had to induce her labor to get him out but, to Tianna, he was the most beautiful thing in the world. Life had been quiet for them since they'd left Michigan and settled in Georgia. The quietness was something they both could appreciate. Tianna walked inside Tiny's hospital room to find her fully dressed and ready to go.

"Bitch, I'm glad you here, I can't wait to get outta here. I need some real food and my own bed. I don't know how they keeping people alive in a hospital serving them food like this," Tiny complained, pointing over to the tray of dry chicken breast and hard mashed potatoes they'd brought her for lunch.

"It's cool baby mama, Imma get you whatever you want to

eat as soon as I get you and my God son home," Tianna informed.

Tiny had given birth to a beautiful baby boy with dimples and a full head of hair. She named him Darden after his father. Tiny couldn't have been happier after finally meeting the beautiful life that had been growing inside her for the past nine months. She'd chosen not to find out the gender of the baby while she was pregnant. So, when she finally looked into the eyes of her son and saw they were the same as Darden's, she knew she had to name their child after him.

Once the nurse brought in Tiny's discharge papers, they were ready to head home. They pulled up to their three-bedroom ranch style home. It was nowhere near as luxurious as the Airbnbs they were used to staying in, but this house was their own, somewhere they could truly call home. After getting Tiny's eighty thousand dollars back from the crew, they put their money together, drove to Georgia and bought their house. With the rest of the money, they started a lip-gloss line and a hair business that turned out to be extremely lucrative, allowing them to never have to resort back to their old way of making money.

It had been a lot of bumps in the road but, now that they'd found their lane, the path was smooth. Tianna and Tiny had been through the worst of times together and still came out on top. They both knew that it was only up from there.

"Mommy, how are we gonna have Christmas without

snow? It doesn't even feel like winter time; it's hot," Lexi uttered.

She'd spent the first eight years of her life with the brutal Michigan winters and couldn't understand how there was no snow in the dead of winter. Here it was, the day before Christmas Eve, and Lexi was getting her dolls together so that they could have a barbeque at the beach. Although she loved her new home, she didn't quite understand the change in climate.

"Because baby, it doesn't snow in Mexico. But it's still Christmas time. I think it's great not to have to put on seventeen layers of clothes just to walk outside," Nakia joked.

"Seventeen, try more like twenty-one," Raphael said, walking into the room.

"Y'all are silly if you walked out the house with those many clothes on. I bet it made y'all look funny," Lexi laughed. She laughed even harder as she pictured her parents with so many clothes on, they resembled Oompa Loompas from the movie *Charlie and the Chocolate Factory*.

"Shoot, we had to keep warm. When me and yo mama was yo age, we had to walk nine miles to school, in fifteen feet of snow. Sometimes even barefoot," Raphael exaggerated.

"Boy what? Who did that? I ain't never even seen fifteen feet of snow. And didn't your parents drive you to school when you were young?" Nakia laughed.

"Mama, how did you and Uncle Jalyn get to school back

in them days when y'all was young?" Lexi asked, looking over at Nakia with the most serious face she could muster.

"Yeah, Nakia, how did y'all get to school wayyyy back in them days?" Raphael laughed so hard, he almost fell over.

"First off," Nakia said, rolling her eyes, "it wasn't no wayyy back in the day. And I took a school bus, just like you and Rashaud did when we lived at the old house."

"A bus, y'all had them? What did they look like?" Lexi asked, surprised.

"See, now I feel like you comin' for me," Nakia laughed. "Yes, we had buses, girl. And they looked just like the ones you used to take. Hell, they probably are the ones you used to take," Nakia chuckled.

"Now, she probably ain't lying about that. Detroit public schools probably still pimpin' them same buses," Raphael laughed.

"Little girl, go get the rest of your things ready so we can go to the beach," Nakia chuckled.

Nakia couldn't help but laugh at the way her daughter was calling her old and being extremely serious about it. Lexi exited the room. Raphael walked over to Nakia, wrapped his arms around her waist and kissed her softly on the lips.

"I love you, old lady," Raphael joked.

"I love you too, old man," Nakia replied, and she meant it. The moment she walked inside that hospital room and saw Raphael lying in the bed and the tubes running through his body, the fear of losing him forever took over. Nothing else mattered after that. Nakia had lost too many people and promised God that if he gave her a second chance with Raphael, she would make it work with him.

Raphael was in a coma for two weeks before he opened his eyes. When he did, the first person he saw was Nakia. The fact she was there with him at his bedside waiting for him to wake up let him know she truly loved him. Nakia was there every single day throughout his recovery, no questions asked. When Raphael was better and finally had his strength back, he and Nakia had the conversation they both needed to have. With no more secrets between them, they were able to become happy again.

The family made their way to the beach, which was only about a three-minute walk from their home. Raphael held the basket of food they were going to put on the grill for lunch. Things were getting back to normal for them as a family, and Nakia was happy about that. She only wished she had her brother there to share it with her. She wrapped her hand around the heart-shaped necklace she never took off. Inside the heart were her brother's ashes. After postponing the funerals of Jalyn and Raphael's parents, they decided to get them all cremated. Nakia had taken Jalyn's ashes and had necklaces made for her and the kids with his ashes inside. It was her way of keeping her brother with them every day.

Raphael placed the food on the grill while Nakia played in the sand with the children. Their family was happy and together again. That was all either of them wanted. Even though they had hurt one another in the past, they had the rest of their lives to make up for it by loving each other correctly.

The End.

Did you enjoy the read?
Let us know how much by leaving us a review on Amazon and Goodreads.

PREVIEW

Keep reading for a preview of…

A Set Up For Revenge

By Ashley Williams

CHAPTER 1

Babygirl

My name was Cameron, but everyone called me Babygirl. From my mother's womb until I was about eight years old, I'd always lived in small places. Due to my father's lifestyle, I'd been in and out of hotels all throughout the states. My father, Jonathan, was a pimp and a drug dealer. Before she was murdered, my mother, Wanda, was an addict but wanted to beat the addiction to crack so bad. At least she acted like it.

Along with being an addict, my mother was very evil. She let my father beat me and even tried selling me to his clients without a care in the world. I can't count how many times I'd ran away, wondering why my mother would do this to me. A mother was supposed to love and nurture her child, and with me being a young girl, one would think that would be my mother's sole purpose. Unfortunately, it wasn't.

Things only went from bad to worse as the years went by and as I grew older. Life became harder, and eventually, tragedy struck. My mother was unintentionally killed by my father. He had shot at an intruder who made his way inside our small home, and my mother was caught in the crossfire as she moved about our dark house to safety. She was shot in her chest and died instantly.

My father was arrested that night but was subsequently acquitted of murder charges after all twelve jurors found him not guilty. If you ask me, he should have gone to jail. The murder may have been an accident, but had my father not been involved with shady people who later became enemies, then maybe my mother would still be alive today. She may have done some dirty things and hurt me in ways no child should ever have to endure, but I still loved her. I thought about her often and found myself envisioning what life would have been like had she loved me just a little bit more.

Alice, one of my father's prostitutes, had been a part of my life for quite some time now and I just loved her. My father had been cheating on my mother with Alice for a while and I knew all about it. As a daughter, my loyalty should've been with my mother and I could've told her about my father and Alice, but with the way she treated me, I really didn't care. Regardless of her dealings with my father behind my mother's back, Alice had always loved and protected me. She never condoned my father mistreating me.

She was more of a mother to me than my biological mother ever was, and I gave her more respect than I could remember giving to my mother. Alice made me feel seen and heard. She made me feel like I was special to her. When my mother died, it made sense for Alice to take on the role as stepmother. A role that she embraced.

I sat in my window on a late, summer night watching the streets, and all I could seem to focus on was my stepmother. I watched her get in and out of cars with strangers, collect money, and stuff it in her bra. At fifteen, I knew what she was doing was wrong, but I would never condemn her in my mind or out loud. The hopping in and out of cars lasted a few hours and I kept watch like her bodyguard in the distance. Not long after she had walked into the house, I could hear my father yelling at her.

"Where is my money hoe? Why is it short?!" His voice echoed through the walls. Alice matched his tone, screaming and hollering, making the situation worse. When I came out of my room my father was dragging Alice through the hallways. I watched as his open hand and closed fist connected with her face. He brutally assaulted her and ripped her clothes from her body. "Bitch, I knew you had my money!" He yelled as he continued his assault with a backhand across her cheek.

Alice always found ways to steal money in order to make sure that I not only had food on the table, but clothes on my back. She knew what she was risking by playing with my father's money, but she did it anyway. After making sure she handed over all of the night's take that she'd worked hard for, my father sent her to her room like she was a child. Satisfied, he left the house, and I immediately ran towards Alice's room. I swung the door open and flew into the room to be by her side. It hurt me to see her hurt.

"Are you okay?"

"Babygirl, I'm okay. You know I'll do anything to take care of and protect you," she proclaimed while holding my hand and looking into my eyes. I felt what she had said was true indeed. I'd always wondered why my stepmother protected me and loved me the way she did when I wasn't really her child. I planned to ask her one day when the time was right.

"Can I get you anything?"

"No Babygirl, just go to your room until I can figure everything out," she replied. I didn't know what she meant by that. I wanted so badly to stay with her in fear that my father would come back for round two, instead I did what I was told.

When he did return back to the house, I could tell that he was both high and drunk. He stood at the entryway of my room and told me he needed to talk to me. I stared up at him with disdain written all over my face as he spoke.

"Babygirl, what Alice did was out of line and I'm sorry you had to witness that. She's been stealing from me, and I finally caught her," he explained. I really wasn't trying to hear it. I knew what she did and didn't care because he deserved it. I sat on the bed and listened to him talk about nothing for a while, making up excuses as to why he needed to teach Alice a lesson, until she walked in. Her eyes were black, her lips busted and bloody.

My father looked over his shoulders and scolded her. "Get the fuck out, you fat bitch!" Him saying that to her broke my heart because I knew he was only being mean and hateful. Alice looked at my father with tear filled eyes and walked away from the door feeling embarrassed, I'm sure. I looked at him with disgust and shook my head. "You get you some rest and I'll see you in the morning." With that, he left my room and I laid my head on my pillow with thoughts of me and my stepmother getting away from him.

In the middle of the night, they were right back at it, but this time I didn't hear my father beating on Alice. I guess he figured she'd had enough. I could hear their heated argument through my halfway opened door. My father threw insult after insult at Alice and I didn't know how she had the strength to sit there and take it.

"Why did you marry me if you didn't accept me as I was, big and all?" I could hear her ask my father.

"I'm still trying to figure that out myself. I'm tired of fussing with you though. If you know like I know, you'll drop this and take yo' ass to bed. I'm still not over the fact that you've been stealing from me and I'm a few minutes off your ass." I only hoped that Alice took heed to what he said and left well enough alone. When I heard no response and saw my father walk past my room towards the back of the apartment, I knew she had.

Relieved, I laid back down and closed my eyes. Before I could get back to sleep, Alice rushed into my room. Her eyes darted around before landing on me. "Pack some of your things, we're leaving." I looked at her and smiled and then looked to my ceiling thanking God for answering my prayers.

Knowing we didn't have much time, I hopped out of bed and scrambled to grab as much of my belongings as I could. Once I was done, she motioned for me to follow her. We ran out of the door as quickly and quietly as possible. Throwing all of our stuff in the backseat of the car, we jumped in and sped off. Never looking back, we left both my father and Louisiana.

We found ourselves in Alice's hometown of Texas, where we moved from hotel to hotel, which was something I was used to. Even if I wasn't used to it, I didn't mind adapting. I was willing to do anything to stay away from my father. Being with Alice, I felt free, and I loved the thought of not having to worry about my father's verbal and physical abuse anymore. That feeling of being free ended all too soon.

One night while I was laying on the bed reading a book, I heard a loud noise. It was so loud, I knew it had to be right outside of our room. I got up from the bed and made my way to the window to see what was going on. My eyes widened when they landed on my father. I watched as he beat on a car window until it shattered. My heart rate sped up when I saw him reach inside the car and pull Alice out. He was yelling so loud, I could hear him all the way in the room.

"Bitch, you thought you could run to Texas, and I wouldn't find you?! You're on my turf and I have people all over this state. Where is Babygirl?" He barked. Alice didn't utter a peep of my whereabouts.

This only infuriated him, causing him to rain down heavy blows on her body. People went about their business as if the scene was a normal occurrence. Scared, I ran and hid in the closet. From the closet, I noticed the hotel door was slightly open. I had planted myself in the closet, frozen in fear. There was no way I could close it and risk being seen by my father.

I was slender in build, so it was easy for me to curl up on the closet floor to hide myself from his sight. The floor in the closet was filthy, but the thought of having to face him made me fight through it. My mind was racing and I had that terrible feeling in the pit of my stomach. I never wanted to feel this way again; at least not this soon. Memories of the night my mother was killed flooded my mind.

What if he killed Alice too? I thought to myself. I couldn't lose her. My thoughts were immediately cut short when I heard him bust into our hotel room. I could hear things being tossed around and concluded that he was trashing the place. It didn't sound like he was looking for me, in fact, he never even called out my name. He had to have been looking for whatever money he thought Alice had and drugs.

I had contorted my body in such a way that when he opened the closet door, he didn't notice me amongst the clothing that hung inside. I silently thanked God because if he had looked down, he would've seen me. Finding nothing, he left. When I heard him slam the front door, I let out a sigh of relief and waited for about five minutes before exiting the closet. Pushing the door open slowly, I picked up on how eerily quiet the room was. All of our belongings were thrown about the room and the mattress was turned over.

Rushing to the window in hopes of finding Alice outside, I panicked when I was unable to locate her. Fishing for my cell phone through the mess my father had made, I went to dial her number and paused. Alice had always taught me to think before I set my mind out to do anything. I knew that if she wasn't here then my dad had taken her and calling would be bad for the both of us. Here I was, a young girl, with no place to go, leftovers in the microwave, a few dirty clothes to put on, and no money.

I thought things like this only happened in movies, but reality had set in really quick that it was happening to me, and I had to accept it. I never knew my grandparents and I highly doubted any of my aunts would want me, so I opted to not call any of them. I was strong for the most part and Alice had taught me how to survive as best she could. I decided that I would wait to see how things played out. Taking my time to put the room back together, I listened to the radio for a while and wondered how many nights Alice had paid to stay in the room. I jumped up after the thought and rushed to the lobby. In such a rush, I almost fell walking in and the man sitting at the front desk giggled a little before asking me if I was okay.

"Yes, I'm fine," I replied, embarrassed. "I'm in room 212, and I need to know how many nights I have left to stay here before I have to pay again?"

"You should know that," he retorted. I ignored his smart comment. I wasn't in the position to go back and forth with this man, so I just waited for his answer. Looking down at the computer, he clicked a few buttons and looked back up at me. "It's paid for eleven more days." I sighed and thanked him, then turned to walk away. "If you need more time, I'm sure we can work something out, if you know what I mean." I heard him say from behind me.

I knew exactly what he meant and when I turned around and saw his creepy eyes staring at me with a mouthful of tobacco, I quickly made my exit. Back in my hotel room, I ran myself a bath to wash off the dirt from the closet as well as the old man's dirty stare. After taking an hour-long bath, I began to think of my next move. In the corner of the room, I eyed Alice's make-up bag, clothes, and Ziploc bag full of condoms. I knew I couldn't fit her clothes, but everything else was a go.

I was still a virgin, but I felt like it couldn't be that hard to use what I had to get what I wanted. Alice had sex for money every night and nothing happened to her. She returned home each night, with tired eyes but for the most part, she seemed alright. I mean, she was right back to it the next night like clockwork. I stood in the mirror, admiring my body, and the thought faded into my imagination. "No way," I thought to myself. "There has to be another way."

The next night as my stomach growled, thoughts of working the streets came back to my mind. With no money and no alternative, I got dressed in heels and the only dress that I packed. I put on red lipstick, put my hair in a high pony-tail, and applied mascara and eyeliner just as I'd seen Alice do plenty of times. To look at the finished work, I grabbed the mirror that was left behind. I was amazed at how different and grown I looked.

Here it was a Thursday night, and I was about to do some-thing I would probably regret later. I took one last glimpse at my innocent face and headed out the door. I didn't know the first place to begin so I turned and walked towards the lobby. The thought of that man at the front desk gave me the shivers, but I kept walking in that direction. Surprisingly when I stepped inside of the lobby, it was a woman standing behind the desk and not the pervert.

"May I help you?" The lady asked with a friendly smile. Looking down at my attire, I put my head down, ashamed, and walked out of the hotel without responding. Stepping outside, I was startled by a tall guy with tattoos that painted his neck. I admired his long beard and muscular frame. Figuring he could be my potential first customer, I shot him a seductive look as if I knew what I was doing.

"How old are you?" He asked.

"Eighteen," I lied. He asked me to get into his car and although hesitant, I followed as he walked in front of me. In my mind I was thinking, wow this is really about to go down. Sitting in the passenger seat, I avoided eye contact with him and went for what I knew and started to touch myself sexually. I leaned over and touched his face, still in disbelief that I was doing such things. I went to reach for the big bulge in between his legs, but he did something unexpectedly; he grabbed my hand.

"Why are you out here doing these things?"

Annoyed, I leaned back in my seat with an attitude. "Look, I'm just out here trying to make some money."

"Why?" He questioned further.

"Because I have to pay for my hotel room and buy food. Is there anything wrong with that, mista?" I clapped my hands at him. He pulled out a few hundreds and handed them to me. "What's the catch? And how can I repay you?" I asked with my eyes big in amazement.

"Just stay out of these streets, that's the catch. Next time, you won't be so lucky and run into somebody like me. You will get what you're looking for from one of these thugs out here." I slowly got out of the vehicle, embarrassed yet again.

How can I be so stupid? This had always worked for Alice, but I wasn't her. Heading back into the hotel, I made me way to my room. I wanted so bad to grab the phone and call Alice but I didn't want to regret calling. My dad may have been waiting by the phone or had her phone, and I couldn't risk it, at least not yet. Mulling over the night's events, I laid down and before I knew it, I was fast asleep.

Available Now On Amazon

OTHER BOOKS BY

URBAN AINT DEAD

Tales 4rm Da Dale

The Hottest Summer Ever

Hittin' Licks For The Holidays: Atlanta

By **Elijah R. Freeman**

Despite The Odds

By **Juhnell Morgan**

Good Girl Gone Rogue

By **Manny Black**

Hittaz

Hittaz 2

Hittaz 3

Coldhearted

By **Lou Garden Price, Sr.**

Charge It To The Game

Charge It To The Game 2

A Summer To Remember With My Hitta

Merry Trapmas: Ice & Frost

By **Mia Sky**

Charge It To The Game 3
By **Nai**

The Swipe 2
By **Toōla**

A Gangsta's Last Kiss
By **Mia Sky**

Pretti & The Beast
By **P. Wise**

Thug Me The Right Way
By **DiamondATL & Nai**

BOOKS BY

URBAN AINT DEAD's C.E.O

<u>Elijah R. Freeman</u>

Triggadale

Triggadale 2

Triggadale 3

Tales 4rm Da Dale

The Hottest Summer Ever

Murda Was The Case

Murda Was The Case 2

Murda Was The Case 3

Hittin' Licks For The Holidays: Atlanta